Out of Darkness

The Lost Library Series
Novella 1.5

Out of Darkness

The Lost Library Series
Novella 1.5

Written by: R.E.Journeys

Cover art by: Natalia Jones

More books by R.E.Journeys:

<u>The Lost Library Series:</u>

From Shadows

Published by R.E.Journeys Creations LLC

www.journeythruthepages.wordpress.com

Copyright © 2021 R.E.Journeys

ISBN 978-1-7368547-8-5

To my grandparents – for your support, for your dreams of a writer in the family, for stapling papers together so I could write stories as a child. I love you all.

Chapter 1

A cool night – quiet, save for the crackling.

The amber glow in the sky tells me he actually did it. I reach the peak of the hill and look out at the village…what used to be a village. Even from here I can feel the change in the air. The warmth from the blaze presses on my face; an uncomfortable feeling for the fall.

More screams sound as hooded figures walk out of a house. They drag a figure out behind them. Someone throws a torch on the house and the figure screams. The wail slices through the silence and the cold distance I've been able to maintain for so long.

I can't do this anymore.

I walk down the hill. The wind blows my cloak and nips my arms. I pull the cloak tighter around me, despite the growing heat.

The crackling grows louder as I enter the village. The heat from the houses already ablaze tells me to lose the extra layer. But I can't. It's our symbol. It's what makes us who we are. Even if I don't know what that is anymore.

I pass the former homeowner, crying in front of his unsalvageable abode. I keep my gaze forward. More shadow people run by, and I know they're looking for the leader of this village. One of the stragglers stops and looks at me.

"Nice of you to join us," the man gripes.

"I had more pressing issues," I say.

"Getting soft-hearted, are we?" he smirks. His teeth glow in the torch light, venomous, waiting for me to falter.

"You wish." I push past him, keeping my head high.

Sweat drips down the back of my neck. I don't need to be here. I shouldn't be here.

"Mommy!" a boy cries out from the street ahead. "Mommy!"

I clench my teeth as his shrieks are cut short.

What have we done?

Another group of cloaked figures run by, laughing. I halt in the shadows of a statue and watch them. They slap each other on the back and run toward an untouched building. A minute later another scream is cut short. That must be why it's so silent.

He gave the order to kill.

My heart trembles, unsure if it wants to keep going. I close my eyes and exhale as I continue my walk. I've got to find him. I just need to find him, give him my report, and leave. I can leave all of this far behind.

I come upon a man holding a torch. Though he is cloaked like the rest of us, his hood is down. The fire from the building in front of him illuminates his figure, his flame red hair looking even wilder in this inferno.

"Ralph," I say.

The man turns his head slightly. "Hey, Kiara."

I stand next to him and stare at the fire. Its flames dance recklessly, putting on a mesmerizing show. It should stir something in me, but I was hollowed out long ago. Ralph gets a good look at me. "Something the matter, K?"

I face him, his green eyes almost hazel in the firelight. I once mistook his ability to read me for concern. Since then, I've learned to never bare anything but my teeth. "Just looking for the chief. You see him?"

"He headed straight for the leader. Since we haven't received any orders to halt this bonfire, I'm guessing the man held out. Shame. This would have been a good place to have a base, you know?"

A base near the southern end of the Steline Mountain range would be secure. I might have been able to request a transfer here. Away from-

More howls of laughter sound from a nearby street.

"Thank you," I say. I leave him to watch his handy work.

An ice wind blows inside of me and I shiver. I just need to find him and I can leave.

I'm sure he has the leader held in one of two places, the center of town or Ephemeral Mine. The mine would be the wise choice. The leader can just open the mine and we can be on our way.

But I know him.

The pair will be in the center of town, so the leader can hear the screams of the townspeople. It's not just a tactic to make the leader cave, Thane likes to watch people suffer. We're far beyond stopping this madness.

I pass another dirt street with more laughter. I'd pass this by, but this kind of group laughter means nothing good is happening. Yes, this whole place is burning in Damned Fire, but there is no reason for this. I turn down the street, walking tall and proud.

My heart pounds, desperate to get away.

I approach the group of hooded men, taking turns kicking a lump on the ground.

"Don't you have anything better to do?" I ask. I keep my chin high, my eyes narrow, just like I've been taught. There is only one way to deal with people who live in the shadows.

"Yes, ma'am," they mutter and run away to continue the destruction of the village. I sigh, but tense back up when one of the men returns, carrying a blazing torch.

"Almost forgot this," the man says, tossing the torch through a window. Once he is sure the fire has caught, he runs off.

The woman on the ground moans, barely registering what is going on around her. I can barely register what is going on around me. The fire flares, climbing out and up the front of the building. Wood houses, dead and burning. Dead…

Something grabs my ankle and I look down. A bloody, dirt-crusted hand grips my boot. The woman shakes as she pulls herself to me, silently sobbing.

"…My baby…" she says. Her voice is hoarse. Only God knows what they did to this woman before I got here. She stares at me, brown eyes alight with fire, with…

I look back at the house.

"Please…" she cries. Another cry sounds from inside the building.

I pull my leg out of her shaky grasp. She stares at me, waiting for me to make up my mind. But I have already decided.

I march away into the night. The woman's shrieks fade as the cool, dark night welcomes me again.

I'll find him later.

Chapter 2

"Again, Kiara."

I sigh and flick my wrist. A polished wooden staff pops out of thin air and into my hand. The strait of the staff is smooth, save for carved symbols with meanings I have yet to decipher. The top forms a loop with four bird wings. The two top wings are folded in, while the bottom two are out, like the bottom set of wings on a butterfly. I don't know why, but Thane says this staff was meant for me, that it's part of me. I rolled my eyes at that comment then and I roll my eyes now.

Once I got the staff, old man Gareth told me I needed to practice this technique. He won't completely explain it to me, but somehow, I can store my weapon in between dimensions, summoning it at will. And it will always appear, no matter where I am. When I asked why it doesn't work for him, he didn't quite elaborate. I just heard him mumble something strange under his breath.

"Good. Now, store it," Gareth says, not looking up from his book.

Gareth has been my tutor for most of my time with Thane. He joined us about a year after I met Thane. I'm not sure what deal he has with Thane, but he is considered one of the most important people here. He has taught me everything – reading to math to the history of Ulterra. When he isn't educating me, he is holed up in what he calls his office. In reality, it's the HQ's library. It has all manner of books.

I do as he says. "Some tutoring session," I respond.

He shuts the book. "This is an invaluable skill Kiara. No one will be able to take it from you when you don't have the staff on you."

I roll my eyes, like I would be in a situation where someone would want to take my staff from me. Thane won't let me go anywhere remotely dangerous. He still treats me like a child.

A hooded figure enters Gareth's study, interrupting whatever retort I had. He hands a note to Gareth, bows, and leaves. Gareth scours the note, frowning the further down he goes.

"Looks like Thane wants to see you," he says, folding up the note. "Off you go."

I clench my jaw. "Thank you," I say as I take my leave.

I hate being treated like a child.

I stomp down the hallway towards Thane's chamber. I pass other members, all of them shrinking as I pass. They know better than to mess with me when I'm in a bad mood.

"Curses! How? How did she do it?"

I enter the inner chamber and kneel. I keep my hood on and eyes on the floor.

"Rise, Kiara," Thane says mid pace. He refocuses on a blurry image before him. "Tell me, how is it the woman who is trapped in some God-forsaken building found *him?*" I stand and remove my hood.

Thane has been looking for this "him" since I can remember. Knowing next to nothing about this matter, I keep my mouth shut. I fix my eyes on the image ahead of me. A boy, no older than me, is climbing a winding path up to a decaying house on a hill. He pauses, staring out at something beyond our sight. He then turns around, squeezes through the fence, and the image fades.

"What was that, sir?" I ask.

"That was the boy we've been looking for. I thought we didn't need him, that everything would work without him, but…gods! All our work!" Thane pounds his fist into the enchanted mirror, cracking it. I control my urge to jump.

"Why do we need *him?*"

Thane smirks. "Jealous, are we, Kiara?"

Thane is the only other person who has been able to read my emotionless face. Unlike Ralph, Thane does care…or at least, he used to.

"Of course not, sir. But you said my power was all we needed to achieve our goal. Are you going to tell me I need him to find my brother too?"

"But *he* would guarantee our success."

I clench my jaw. The unspoken part is that I do need him to find my brother. I loathe being in debt to anyone else, not when we are so close.

"Of course, there is an alternative," Thane continues.

"What are your orders, sir?" I stare at my reflection in the fractured mirror. Thane begins pacing back and forth again. It's his favorite thing to do when he's thinking. Though sometimes I suspect he does it to torment me. He loves watching people writhe, the nerves getting the better of them. I admit I enjoy it too, when he's doing it to others.

Thane mutters something into his hands and holds it out toward the mirror. The image returns, though distorted from the crack. I watch the boy, who is now in a terribly dark room, only illuminated by a tame fire. He stands up and falls back down into a chair. He continues to fidget in his seat. Light engulfs the room and clears, revealing just the old woman, mouth moving, sitting across from an empty chair.

"So, it's begun." Thane says, glowering at the mirror.

That flash of light stirs a memory. Something familiar perhaps?

"Where did he go?" I ask.

Thane marches over to a covered book case. He unlocks the murky door, eyes me to make sure I haven't moved, and pokes through it. I hear him ruffle through pages of some old book. He groans, slams the book shut, and locks the cabinet.

"You ready to use your gift, Kiara?"

"My gift, sir? You mean-"

"Yes," his golden eyes light up, "we're going on a field trip, to visit a friend of mine."

Chapter 3

I stand back, panting as Thane talks to some creepy old King. I've practiced opening portals before, but we've never traveled together. Old man Gareth has gone with me before – always into a children's book, about ducks or cookies. Just like Gareth, Thane held my arm, like a gentleman escorting a lady to dance, and didn't let go until we came out.

The old man's solid black eyes shift to me once and a while as the pair mumble to each other. I narrow my eyes in threat to the old man. I can take him.

"You can't be serious," the King mutters, breaking the string of unintelligible words between the two.

"I'm afraid I am," Thane responds. "But don't worry, I know you can destroy them. He's weak and out of his element."

"Are you sure you don't want him?"

"No. Kill him and anyone who dares to oppose you." Thane's anger is cool and sends a shiver down my spine. He turns to me and I straighten.

"But you reme-"

"Kill him," Thane snaps. "He'll ruin everything." My ears twitch.

"As you wish, Your Highness," the King bows, a twisted expression dancing across his face.

Thane ignores him. "Come Kiara, it's time to go back." He grabs my arm again as I open the portal. I glance back at the King and his smile feels like sleet on my skin. We enter the vortex and head back to HQ.

〰◆〰

"You all did very well," Thane says. "We have acquired all the needed quartz thanks to the contribution from the Ephemeral mine."

We've been in our meeting hall for our weekly HQ meeting. Hooded figures stand in uniform, listening with rapt attention to Thane's latest monologue.

The room erupts in cheers. I shift and glance across the dais at Ralph. He remains as stoic as ever. Thane raises his arms and the room falls silent.

"There will be a celebration tomorrow night for your hard work," Thane says.

Everyone claps and shouts.

"Alright, you've all got jobs to do. Dismissed."

The room empties in a manner of minutes, leaving me with Thane and Ralph. Thane stalks back to his throne and throws himself down. He removes his hood to reveal a smug smile.

"That went well, don't you think?" He turns his head toward Ralph.

"Very well, sir," Ralph responds, crossing his arms.

His red hair is considerably less intense inside the cavernous meeting hall. No windows and only a few torches light the room. I watch the nearest torch dance, defiant of the little space it has been given to move.

"What do you think, Kiara?"

"Sir?" I ask, pulling myself from the flame's mesmerizing movements.

"Our mission at Ephemeral Mine, it went well, didn't it?" Thane asks, his golden eyes molten in the torch light.

"Y-yes, very well. How much quartz did we get?" I ask.

"Several carts full, not as much as I wanted, but it will suffice," Thane waves, clearing the air around his head.

Suffice? That's all he has to say on it? People died. Children turned to orphans, husbands and wives forever separated by death. And what we took from them will only *suffice.*

"What a disgusting look you have there," Ralph says. "Wait, no that's your natural face." He smirks.

I bite back a few choice words for him. "Thane, why did we have to kill the villagers?" Thane raises an eyebrow, so I add, "Wouldn't they have been more useful to us, alive?"

He smiles. "Oh Kiara, sometimes you have to squash a few cockroaches if you want to get the kitchen running. Don't worry. If you want your own squad, there are plenty of people we can recruit."

I open my mouth several times, but I can't think of anything useful to say. Anything that I want to say will come across as treasonous. I watch as Thane and Ralph leave the room. This isn't the Thane I know. The Thane I know wouldn't kill the innocent. He would protect them with his very life. He promised me, the day we created Gemini, that we would protect people.

Thane reaches the doorway and glances back at me before exiting.

Something twists inside me.

He fears this *boy* and wants him dead. Maybe I'll see to it this boy comes out of the story alive, even if it means facing the creepy old man. Then maybe, just maybe I can stop this new Thane and get the old one back.

Chapter 4

I step out into a green haze. My pulse is racing and I'm just about out of energy. I keep my chin up though. I can't show weakness, especially to a demon, even if he looks like an old man. Thane, after some prodding, told me about Cantorn, the demon of chaos and misery. The problem is I can't stay here too long. One reason is because Ralph will be looking for me for a training session soon. The second reason is, without Thane, I have no protection against Cantorn's powers.

"Well, well, what do we have here?" the King mocks in his disturbing, dual voice.

"Change in plans," I respond. "Thane wants them to survive."

"He didn't say that, did he, little girl?" His smile grows too wide to be natural.

I narrow my eyes. "He did. Thane has devised a new plan and it requires the boy's survival." I look out at three figures, struggling to stand.

My mother told me that people who are overcome by misery can end up on the floor, unable to move. Even now I can feel the misery threatening to pull me down.

"Can I play with them a little bit before sending the boy back to your world?" Cantorn licks his lips.

"Do as you will," I say, turning around to leave. I look out one last time and see the boy staring at me. I shift my weight.

What's wrong with me? He can't see me through this fog. The boy is going to have to deal with this himself. I open a vortex and head back to HQ. Cantorn starts talking as the portal closes.

He's impossible.

〜💧〜

"Thane's been looking for you."

I step into the hall, shutting my room door behind me. I collapsed in there as soon as the portal closed. I've been sleeping for who knows how long. There are no windows in a cave dwelling, a major downside in using a cave as a HQ.

"Well, I've been in my room," I say.

"We knocked," Ralph says, pushing himself off the wall.

I walk down the hall towards Thane's chamber. "Sorry, I must have been sleeping. That whole 'portal to a story world' thing makes me tired."

"He's not there," Ralph calls out.

I stop and turn around, glaring. "Then, where is he?"

"Gone," Ralph smiles. That man loves getting a rise out of people.

"Where, Ralph?" I raise an eyebrow.

"He's heading for Lummava as we speak. He's going to do some recruiting in the area. He wanted his right-hand gal there with him." I growl at him. He dares call me *gal*? He smiles.

"Are you coming or am I to travel alone?" I pray for the latter.

"Your carriage awaits, milady." Ralph bows. His sarcasm will be the death of him.

I walk back the other way. He stands as I pass him.

Or at least he thought I was passing him. I reach up to push his head into the wall, but a gust of wind flies out instead. The earthen wall cracks as he pulls himself out. He groans rubbing the back of his head. I keep walking, hiding my shocked expression, my heart pounding. I've never done that before. I resist the urge to look at my hands. My mind scatters, searching for something to shield my panic.

I smile.

At least now he'll remember who he is speaking to.

Chapter 5

Ralph and I arrive in Lummava via hired coach. "Only the best for the princess," Ralph mocked when we stepped into the carriage.

The night flew by without a word between the two of us, at least not about the sudden magic. I tried to get some sleep, but the excitement of visiting other towns was just too much. Now, I regret it. I'm exhausted, but I'm here.

Lummava is full of energy and excitement. There are shops, bakeries, and people just going about their business. I'm sure there is at least one bookstore here. My heart leaps at the thought. If I didn't work with Thane, I think I would like to live in a town like this.

I wander forward, hood up and face concealed. Ralph grabs my arm and whispers, "The recruiting will be in a half hour, don't wander too far."

"Yeah, yeah." I wave him off. I snort in disbelief. Thane actually thinks I need a babysitter if he left Ralph behind to wait for me. What kind of trouble am I going to get into? Unless…No. Thane can read me, but he doesn't know everything.

I saunter around, looking at the festivities in the town square. This place is certainly livelier since the last time I visited. Before it was grey and empty, a one-horse town. But now, this seems to be the place to be. I love it.

Lummava has always felt familiar, like I belong here. I'm never more at ease then when I'm here. That's why, when I was heading back from my last mission, I stopped in.

I stop near a fountain and listen to some performers by the fountain, playing a moving piece. They are spectacular, using a mixture of piano and forte, high and low notes, and different types of instruments to portray a battle between many groups. How I wish I could listen to them longer, but my half hour is going to burn up fast and I have an errand I want to run.

When I stopped in last time, I ran into an old man who spilled plants everywhere. I helped him gather his items and he invited me for tea. I can't pass up a good tea, and based on the herbs he was carrying, I could tell this man knew a good tea from dish water. We sat and talked for hours. He is such a kind person, the first person I was able to open up to about everything, including Thane and Gemini.

Thane never told me why he called it Gemini. Maybe because it started with the two of us? Of course, that doesn't matter. We could call ourselves anything we wanted; the public will always call us Shadow Dwellers. Our grey gradient cloaks don't really help the matter.

I turn into the alley where Heinz's herb shop is located. The tall buildings block sunlight from reaching the alley, casting everything in an all too familiar darkness.

I try to look over my shoulder, but my hood blocks my view. I roll my eyes. I feel like someone has been following me since the musical performance, but I can't see past my hood. Whatever, it really doesn't matter. If it's another member they can tell Thane anything they want. The man knows I love my tea. I ran out of herbs for that tea Heinz makes and I have been itching to get back here since.

I enter the shop, and a tiny bell sings, announcing my presence. I look around and take a deep breath. This shop smells so wonderful. Lemongrass being the dominant smell, I believe.

"Hello?" an old man calls out. "I'm back here."

Is the man daft? I told him last time not to say that. I could easily pocket the herbs I need and be out of here without him ever seeing me. I shake my head, calming my rising irritation. Heinz doesn't deserve it.

I march forward, past the tall shelf displays and towards the back counter. This place is so crowded with drying plants. Heinz really needs a better method in organizing all of this.

"Hey, Heinz," I say when I finally see the old man. It looks like he has been washing off some new product. Heinz slams a wooden crate on the counter, full of herbs ready to be hung to dry. He coughs and I swear I could hear a bell ring.

"Kiara, you're here! I'm so happy!" He beams.

"Yes, of course I am. I did promise I would come back to visit," I say. The happy calm in my voice is foreign to me. "How have things been going?"

"Pretty good, I think. I had a lot of travelers from the FHB stop in to get some herbs for their next job today. Oh, to be young and adventuring," Heinz sighs and his eyes grow misty. Whatever this man did in his early years must have been grand. Even with his wrinkles and sun spots, I can see he has quite a few old scars. I wonder if he was a member for the Fortune Hunters Bureau, or FHB for short.

"What are you talking about? Having your own shop is an adventure." I smile at him.

I think I would like to work in a shop like this. It'd be fun to prepare the products, clean the shop, organize, and deal with customers. I know others would find it boring, but a quiet shop out of the hustle and bustle of the world stage is what I've longed for. It's the consistency I've longed for.

"I guess you could say that," Heinz responds wistfully. "So, what about you? Are you still working with that one group?" His voice is sincere, but my heart tears when he asks.

"Y-yes." I look away, ashamed. So much has happened since I last saw him. Heinz stares at me with concern. "It's a good job. I'm…helping people. We are going to change the world."

"You seem so sad though. Do you not agree with this man?" Images of Ephemeral burning, the screams being cut short in the night dance through my vision. Why did Thane snap that night?

"Those poor people…" I whisper as I remember the woman crying for her child.

"What was that dear?" he asks me.

"Oh! No! Everything is fine," I say, waving my hands. "We will make the world a better place. I know it. Now about the herbs I need…" I study his face. He pushes his stool back, coughing as he stands. I swear I hear the bell ring again. I must be imagining things.

"Ah, the herbs for the tea, right?" Heinz winks. "I gave you a year supply and it's only been…a month?"

"Yes," I flush.

Heinz lets out a laugh. A genuine, worry free laugh. "Of course, how about I get you two years supply this time? That should last you two months, at most."

"Ha, ha, very funny, Heinz," I smile in defeat.

I help Heinz gather the necessary herbs and hand him some money.

"No, no, dear, it's on me," Heinz pulls his hands up.

"Heinz, I couldn't," I say in earnest.

"From one tea lover to another. Just promise me you'll visit again. I love our chats." He hands me a sack with the herbs.

I choke down a sob. No one has ever done something so kind for me. "Thank you, Heinz. And of course, I will visit again – you don't need to bribe me with herbs."

"Of course, I do," he chuckles, "I can't have you getting herbs from any other shop."

"I would never," I smile, feigning hurt that he would suggest such a thing.

We laugh together and then Ralph's comment comes back to me.

"Heinz, I've got to go. Please take care," I say. "And thanks again for the herbs. No one makes a tea like you."

He says goodbye as I disappear into the thick of the shop and out the door. The sun is getting low. It's almost time for the recruiting rally. More like brain washing session.

I walk out of the alley, making sure the herbs are hidden in my cloak's inner pocket. Just because I don't care about Thane knowing about the herbs, doesn't mean I want him to find out where I got them.

A crowd has gathered near the fountain, a loud voice shouting out to all of them. I sigh, so it begins.

Once Thane is done talking, he briskly leaves the stage. Others take his place and the crowd disperses. No riots like the other towns. I guess that's good.

Someone then catches my eye. The boy from the mirror, wearing the same brown jacket, takes a step toward the registration line. He hesitates and wanders over to a bench and sits down, rubbing his hands on his face. The hurt on his face is so familiar. Maybe it's because I've seen it mirrored on so many others. My heart twinges.

A group of kids passes by, talking about games to play. It's a diverse group, but all wearing similar melancholy faces. Something inside me urges me to talk to the kids. I walk up to them.

"What's wrong?" I ask.

"We lost our ball," the elf boy says.

"Well, that's not good. Can't do anything without a ball." I reach my hand into an outer pocket.

"What's that?" the dwarf girl asks.

"A ball," I smile wryly. A wave of my hand and the tiny ball enlarges. It's a magic toy of some sort. It hasn't worked in a while, so I'm glad it's working now. Thane thought I would like it when I was younger. Maybe they'll like it too.

A human boy asks, "Can we play with it?" His eyes go wide in anticipation of my answer.

"Of course," I say, holding it out for them. The human girl reaches for it and I snatch it back. "Only if you do two things for me." They nod. "One, be very careful, you don't want to lose this ball too. I don't have another one. And two, keep a good eye on each other." They smile, seeing how simple their end of the bargain is.

"Ok!" the girl shouts. I hand her the ball and she starts levitating it. She's a magicite, and a pretty talented one for her age.

The children take off running and laughing. This is what life should be like. Not the grey, depressing, magic-less world it was just yesterday. That makes me wonder why Thane was so upset.

"Kiara, Thane's ready to go. He's waiting for you," Ralph says as he approaches me. A knowing smirk is plastered on his face.

"Yeah, thanks," I say, not looking at him. The children's laughter rings out, lost behind the long line of people wanting to sign up with Gemini.

I let out a silent sigh and turn to follow him to the carriage. Yes, life is better like this.

Chapter 6

"What is going on, Kiara? Ralph tells me you have something you might want to share." I keep my gaze out the carriage window. That bastard, I knew he would tell Thane. What a crybaby. I send thoughts of pain toward the man sitting with the driver. Stupid Ralph.

"I'm not sure what he is talking about," I respond. I bat my eyelashes, feigning innocence. I'm sure it's about our little encounter at HQ. There's no way he knows about…

"Ralph says you might have been holding your powers a secret," Thane's golden eyes glow a honey yellow. Relief washes over me. Yes, it is about that incident, and by the looks of it, Thane's happy. What a twisted man.

"Oh! Yes," I say, "well, Ralph was accidently on the receiving end of a wind gust that kind of generated from my palm. Can you believe that? Thank goodness he's ok." As much as I hate this childish act, I can't help it around Thane.

Something about him brings it out of me. He's like the big brother I lost so long ago.

My heart skips a beat in memory of Ewan. I don't know what happened that night, years ago, but he just disappeared without warning. I'm thankful Thane found me by chance. Who knows what would have happened to me?

"My, this is exciting news," Thane says, his eyes still twinkling. "We must start training this new skill as soon as we can. I bet there is no limit to your power." He smiles that irksome, knowing smile. It's like he knows every move I make and is toying with how long it takes for me to figure things out.

"Training?" I'm not very fond of our training sessions. But this could be more fun than opening and closing portals into different stories. That is just exhausting.

Thane looks out the window, at the land we are leaving behind. He can't see the looming mountains to his left, telling us where Klenover, the King's city, is. We are still several hours from HQ, and the sun just set.

"Yes, I think it could be useful," Thane rests his chin on his hand as he looks at me. He's calculating the use to him, not to me. He's definitely not like Ewan, but he's all I have. Especially when the only other person I'm close to is that rat, Ralph.

"Sounds good, Thane," I respond. I turn back to the window and watch the landscape roll by. We don't say another word about it.

≈ ◆ ≈

"Kiara! Get in here!" Thane's voice echoes through the hall.

Ralph shifts in his spot and smirks. He loves seeing people get into trouble. I snarl at him and push open the heavy oak doors to the chamber, Thane's office.

"Yes, Thane," I say.

Thane is facing the mirror again, though it seems to have been repaired. Ralph snickers as he closes the doors behind me. I stick my tongue out at him before returning my attention back to Thane.

"Tell me what I'm looking at," Thane says.

I sigh. It's time to tell Thane what he already knows. I hate when he's like this.

I saunter up next to him and fold my arms, eyeing him. I face the mirror and eyes go wide by what I see. The boy is running through the woods with a young man, two lavender skinned elves, and what appears to be a Va'ahn. I've never seen one, but I read about them in one of my many study sessions with old man Gareth. There aren't many Va'ahn's

30

around, though I guess it makes sense seeing him in a story. They are supposed to have infinite knowledge about everything.

"Well," I say carefully, "it looks like a group of people, well beings, running through a thick forest."

"Yes," Thane smiles, "and…"

"Well, they're probably running from something. Or after something. Though, by the look on the guy with glasses, it's probably from something." I smile at Thane.

He pinches the bridge of his nose as he turns around. He starts pacing near his work table. "Does the boy look familiar?" He gestures at the mirror with his free hand, still with his back toward me.

I look at the image again. The group has stopped and are trying to catch their breath. The boy who faced off against Cantorn is amongst the group and I glare. I can't stand the sight of the boy.

"That boy, he's from *Dream and Disappointment*," I say.

"Yes, and that is where he was supposed to stay. What do you think happened?" Thane asks.

He can't possibly know what I did.

"Looks like he beat the old man and got out." I face Thane.

"There is no way he should have beaten Cantorn. The demon should have roasted him instantly. Though I'm sure he would want to play games with them first." Thane chuckles to himself.

"What are we going to do, Thane?" I ask. Best to divert his current line of thought, lest it end with my treason.

"*We* are going to do nothing. You are going to train with Ralph and I am going to take care of this, myself." Thane picks up something on the table and rubs it a few times before it starts sparkling.

"What are you going to do?" I ask.

"Don't worry about it," Thane responds. "Go get Ralph. You need to train before you blow holes through every wall here." Thane waves his hand dismissively.

I stomp out the door and pull it closed behind me. Shimmer stone lamps line the dark hallways.

I've got to do something to stop Thane. Helping the boy brought some good back to the world. If Thane succeeds with his plan, I'll have to deal with a world of grey again. But what can I do?

I kick a pebble and glance at Ralph's shoes.

"Let's go," he says.

I run into Thane's office panting, partly from running here, partly from my heart stopping, and the rest from training with Ralph.

Provocation is that man's favorite method of training. Between taunts and wind bursts, or the lack there of, he mentioned that Thane was going to travel into this story, *A Seed of Courage*, on his own and take care of the boy himself. The shock sent a large wind gust, throwing Ralph into a wall and knocking him out cold. Then, I ran.

First of all, that could kill Thane, something I don't want. And secondly, I'm not ready for the world to go back to grey. Thane has to know what we are doing is killing the world. He has to. Just the little bit of magic that has returned is proof enough that Ulterra needs magic.

I wave my hand in front of the mirror saying Thane's name. An image swirls into focus. A dark, rock hallway is revealed. If I didn't know any better, it could be one of the many halls here at HQ.

Thane, well a hooded Thane, is walking next to a short, scarcely-haired, green goblin. A golden circlet adorns her head, resting on her long, pointed ears. She wears a lush, regal robe that just touches the ground. Based on the occasional bobbing of their heads they appear to be deep in conversation.

They round a corner and a large, rock chamber opens before them. Tiny creatures, goblins I bet, dance around to the beat of an unheard song. Thane and the goblin continue to talk as they observe the scene below. Thane says something that causes the goblin to nod, her gold mini-hoop earring swaying with the motion.

Thane glances over his shoulder and I take a step back. There's no way he can tell I'm watching him. He can't. I wave my arm in the opposite direction, killing the image, and leave his study with less fervor than I arrived. I look around the empty hallway and rush back to my room.

I don't know what Thane is doing, but I need to stop him. I close the door and still my breaths. I need to plan before I do this.

Ralph is going to regain consciousness soon enough. That shouldn't be a problem. Thane won't care since it was a training accident. But Ralph is going to be looking for me. He'll want to train again so he can pummel me.

I run around my room grabbing various items that I think will help me on this journey. I pick up *A Seed of Courage,* fingering through pages and notes to read up on what part of the story Thane is hiding. Thane always said this story was important, so I've read it a few times. I can't let anyone see me once I'm there, but I have to make an impact. That boy is no match for Thane.

〰◆〰

I step out of the vortex in front of a cave, hoots and hollers echoing out of the entrance.

"Close enough," I mutter under my breath.

I charge into the cave, ignoring the dank smell that reminds me of our HQ. Lallie, the Goblin Queen, if I remember, and the others must be in the main room. My eyes narrow, Lallie is going to be tough. I don't know if that boy can face her. Besides, Thane had to have given Lallie another advantage. She gets defeated by, what's his name again?

Lucan. Right.

I stumble on the uneven ground, slowing my pace for a second. So, what was the hero's advantage against Lallie?

A charm!

That's it. But Thane wouldn't have interfered with the main character. No, he makes his deals with devils.

I should have entered around the time of the big fight between Lucan, with his new found ally, Kilbur, and Lallie's forces.

I slow down as I approach a light coming from a chamber up ahead, the sounds of fighting tell me I've found the right place. I crouch low and stalk into the room. Thane is gone and Lallie is making a retreat up the stairs, frustrated about something.

I duck behind some boulders around the perimeter and peer out through a gap. A monster of a man roars, throwing goblins every which way. Knights, mercenaries, and the group I saw from *Dream and Disappointment* are fighting everyone. For every knight that gets knocked down, two more mercenaries stand in their place. This fight is getting nowhere fast.

Lallie reaches the rock balcony, the same one Thane was standing on just minutes ago. She's getting ready for something. I pull out a charm I got from old man Gareth. He gave it to me after a particularly rough training session with Ralph. He must have felt bad for me, though he claims that he's more concerned for the brain he's worked years on teaching.

I hold the shell looking charm and wait for Lallie's attack.

"ENOUGH!" Lallie yells, whipping her hands in the air.

I rub my thumb in a spiral pattern on the shell and whisper, "protection."

A small bubble of a shield forms around me as the edges of her spell wash over me. I sigh in relief. Everyone else is less fortunate, as they are tossed into the air and thrown on top of each other. That definitely would have blown my cover.

Grunts and pains and strained whispers sound from the group in the center of the room, all glued in place. After several futile attempts to move, everyone gives up. I shake my head. No one has a clue about how powerful Lallie really is.

Something catches the boy's attention and I follow his line of sight. I keep staring toward where the large man fell.

Is someone moving?

Someone, considerably smaller than the behemoth, pulls himself out from beneath him.

Oh God, it's Lucan!

"What is this?" Lallie asks. "You shouldn't be able to move! What magic is this?"

Thank God Lucan still has his charm. He should be impervious to Lallie's magic. But then what did Thane do? The goblins appear normal and Lucan has his charm.

Lucan starts pulling on one of the elves, the one on top of the boy, but she's not moving. This is normal too. No one should be able to move until Lallie breaks the spell.

Lallie starts shouting something, which is met by more shouts from various people.

"Well, that's not nice," a creature says from nearby. "I know my visit was cut short, but we were having so much fun. I came all the way out here to visit and you completely ignore me. How terribly rude!"

The creature is a peachy-tan, and about the size of a Great Dane. The Va'ahn! He's here! I've never seen one in person before. He keeps talking to the goblins, so articulate and proper. He then turns and runs out of the cave.

I look back at the angry Lallie. I'm going to get a better view, when shouts accompanied by the stomping of hundreds of feet start growing louder. I duck lower as the tribal goblins take off after the creature.

Strange. That's not supposed to happen. That idiot must have changed something here. I growl in frustration, despite myself. Now there's no way to tell what Thane changed.

Everyone left in the chamber stands, staring up at Lallie who is still throwing a tantrum. At least that's still the same. I roll my eyes.

The change is going to happen soon. But what is it? What…No. There is something the idiot boy couldn't have changed. Which means…

"Kilbur, friends, my offer still stands. In light of the new additions, I can double, even triple the reward. Just think about it for a second," Lallie smiles.

Everyone in the center of the room looks at each other in silent conversation. That's what Thane did. A wide grin spreads on the behemoth's face.

Kilbur rams Lucan, straight into the idiot boy, sending them both flying into the wall. Gravel falls from a higher rock. My heart is racing. How? No. How?

The lot then starts a ridiculous chase, splitting into two groups.

My mind is scanning through every possible scenario. Lucan can't stand up against Kilbur. No, he won't gain his confidence until he confronts Lallie. If Lucan can be confident now, I'm sure he could think of something to stop Kilbur. But as it is now, years of torment have given Kilbur the edge over the hero.

I frantically dig through my cloak pockets. Nothing, nothing, nothing! Uggh! Everything I have is useless. A quill, a hair tie, a shimmer stone, what was I thinking when I grabbed all of this? I peek back out and see the elves have stopped running and have started fighting the mercenaries and knights. The twins masterfully dodge each punch and every kick, responding in kind. They are dominating the group, but there are so many people attacking them, there is no way they can hold out.

On the other side of the chamber, the boy and Lucan split up, Kilbur chasing after the idiot. The boy turns around, a stupid smirk on his face. Kilbur charges him like a raging bull. The boy dives to the side. He clearly hasn't had a lick of training. I shake my head and try to think of a way to help him out of this mess.

The boy stands and sprints away. He's looking every which way for something. He's got to defend himself, at least long enough for Lucan to succeed. Meanwhile, Lucan is running back and forth, dodging plates, goblets, and other items Lallie is throwing at him.

This is pathetic. This is the hero? I know he is overcoming a lot of fears and what not, but seriously? I used to admire him for his courage, and I still do, but this sight has been seared into my memory. The Chicken Boy Hero, that's what they should have called him.

I look back at the idiot I'm supposed to be helping. Or should I help him? If I can somehow help Lucan succeed, maybe I can leave the boy to fend for himself. All that needs to happen is for Lucan to succeed for magic to be released.

A shout pulls me back to the present and the boy falls. He turns over and scrambles away from Kilbur. His gaze is frozen on the monster, but he is still feeling around for…something. That's it. I look around and find a discarded shield a little way away. It'll have to do.

I concentrate, trying to summon a wind strong enough to blow the shield my way. I crawl towards it, trying to close some of the distance. A small wind picks up. I glance up at Lallie to make sure she hasn't noticed. Fortunately, she is still preoccupied with Lucan. I take a risk I'm loathing to do. With a quick gust, the shield rattles toward me. I grab it and rush to the other side of my hiding spot.

Kilbur is getting terribly close the boy. If he gets the idiot, it'll be the end of him, and probably the end of my undercover mission. The thought of outwardly opposing Thane sends chills up my spine. I roll the shield out as Kilbur is bending down, his eyes blind with rage.

The boy grips the shield and swings, knocking Kilbur back a few steps. The boy and I sigh in relief. He examines the shield and stands up. He turns back toward the wall and the boulders. He stares in confusion.

I quickly pull my cloak close to me, my heart pounding in fear. That was close. Kilbur approaches the boy and mindlessly starts punching the shield.

I have to get out of here while I still have the chance. Quietly and carefully, I retreat toward the entrance of the cave. The boy's going to have to take it from here.

〜◆〜

I slump into my bed as someone starts pounding on the door to my room.

"Go away," I mumble. I turn so I can bury my face in the covers.

"Kiara, I just want to talk," Thane says from the other side of the door. I groan. "Kiara?"

I grumble and push myself off my bed. My hood is off and I know my hair is a mess. I glance at my mirror to ensure there is no evidence of me being anywhere otherworldly. A pale faced, frizzy haired old woman stares back at me, dark rings under her green eyes. I sigh and shrug. There's really nothing I can do about how I look. Maybe Thane will let me sleep when he sees how bad I look.

I open the door and glare at the man on the other side.

"Kiara, Ralph tells me your skills are improving. Do you have the energy to show them to me?" Thane smiles his proud big brother smile.

I blink, still exhausted from my latest story excursion.

He continues smiling, a true and curious smile.

"Ok," I say. "Then I am sleeping until eternity."

"Of course," he responds as he leads the way to the training room.

〰◆〰

"Again!" Ralph shouts.

I groan and stomp my foot. An hour. An hour's nap and I was hauled back to the training room.

Apparently, Thane found some book or got some grand notion that if I can summon wind, the other elements "must" be at my command. Now, Ralph has set the room up with fire – pots, candles, and lanterns – testing if I can manipulate the flames, combine them, and then relight everything.

"Stop your griping," Ralph smirks. I stare at him. He got way too much pleasure marching into my room and pulling me from my bed. Since when was eternity only an hour?

Ralph rubs his head without much thought. I widen my stance and hold my hands in front of me, and smirk. "How's the lump treating you?" I ask.

Ralph sneers at me. If I have to be miserable, he will be too.

"Again!" a shout interrupts our banter and ices my heart.

Ralph and I look at each other with wide eyes. I feel flames of fury marching down the hall toward the training room. We remain frozen, waiting for the inevitable.

The training room doors are thrown open and Thane, ablaze with anger, stomps in, seething over something. Ralph and I stare at him.

"You," he points at me, "With me." Thane then stomps away. I look back at Ralph, but there is no trace of amusement on his face. I gulp and leave the room.

Thane leads the way down the hall and back to his work room. My mind runs through possible scenarios and lies for each of them.

There is only one reason he is angry, the boy escaped the story, freeing more magic, which explains my ability to somewhat manipulate fire. There are two possibilities he's called me, because I'm his right hand and the only person who is fully aware of his plans and his mirror, or because he found out about my traitorous activities. If it's the latter, three possibilities of how this could end. One, he kills me as soon as we enter the room. Two, he gives me a chance to prove my loyalties. And three, I break and fight my way out of here.

I don't want to turn against him, I just want to buy myself some time to show him why what we're doing is wrong. Or it's at least the wrong way to go about it. There is another way to achieve the "Era of Peace and Happiness", the thing we proclaim when we go into towns and villages.

We reach the wooden doors to his study and I take a deep breath. The torches on either side flicker as he swoops by and into the room. I follow him inside, leaving the door open in case I do need to run.

"Shut the door," Thane says.

There goes that option. I obey, trying to figure out if I can burn my way out of here. Doubtful, seeing how I'm sure I am imagining my manipulation of flames.

"Thane, what's going on?" I ask.

"Look," Thane says, gesturing at the mirror.

I step up next to him and examine a town at sundown. There are all sorts of people wandering around. Not just people, creatures, goblins…oh…

I clench my jaw as I stare. "Are those goblins?" I ask.

"Yes, they are," Thane looks toward me with an eerie calm.

"Where did they come from?" I ask, keeping my gaze on the mirror.

"Lallie has failed me," Thane responds, looking back at the scene.

Despite it being night, I can tell the town is full of vibrant color. People – no, beings – are wandering around, laughing and enjoying the calm and cool night. A chill runs through me.

"What are we going to do?"

"I will take care of it. You will return to training until Ralph dismisses you."

My heart drops upon hearing this. It's going to be a long night.

I close my eyes. "Is that all?"

"Yes."

I turn and head for the training room, closing the chamber doors behind me. He's going into another story.

Another villain, another plan, and another time I have to help the idiot.

I stop and punch the wall.

What am I doing? Life was so much easier when I didn't bother with this. I trained, I traveled, I read, and I slept. But now, now I'm going to have to double my efforts.

I take off down the hall with my shoulders squared and chin held high. I'll master fire tonight, then I'll figure out what Thane is planning.

Chapter 7

"Dammit, Kiara!" Ralph shouts. I laugh darkly.

Flames from the cauldron by Ralph reach out for him. The sleeve of his cloak catches fire, causing him to rip the whole thing off and stamp the fire out. His toned muscles glisten with sweat.

"Are we done now," I yawn.

"No, you haven't mastered fire, yet," he sneers.

"It's not gonna happen."

He picks up his cloak, examining the damage. "And why is that, Your Highness?"

My skin prickles at the phrase. "Ralph, I. Am. Tired."

"So am I, but we aren't leaving until you have this down."

Something rages inside me. I hold my arms out in front of me and push my hands together; an unknown force making it difficult. The flames of the cauldrons on either side of Ralph start leaning towards him. He looks up from his ruined cloak and sees the flames.

He reaches behind him and chucks a few throwing knives at me. I stop what I'm doing and summon some wind to disrupt the blades path. The knives clatter to the ground.

We glare at each other.

"You keep that up, I'll never dismiss you," Ralph holds his chin up.

Everything inside of me freezes. I could knock him out again, but I'm sure Thane will pull me back here to see my progress. Besides, I might kill Ralph if I hit him again. I grind my teeth.

"Keep that up and you'll have no more teeth."

I scream. I focus again on my task, take the fire from everything, combine it, and redistribute it.

Damn, it's hot in here.

Ralph crosses his arms and watches me struggle. I shoot him a glare once and a while as I try to get the damn flames to move.

A mischievous look dances in his eyes. "I bet that boy could do it," Ralph snickers.

Something inside me snaps and the fires flare, bits of flame flying off to join together in the center. For once, Ralph's teasing is working. I continue focusing on my rage, causing flames to leave their holders and add to the growing fireball in the center of the room. This is it! I'm almost there!

Once all the holders are out of fire, I concentrate on the giant fireball. The fire growls as it continues to weave amongst itself, maintaining a spherical shape. All that's left is to relight everything.

I focus on a cauldron beneath the flare. I command the flames to redistribute themselves, but they aren't obeying. Panic floods me and I struggle to maintain the raging beast in the center of the room. The flames dance and play, trying to go everywhere, but where I want them. My frustration grows as I realize I am spending most of my energy maintaining the blaze in the center of the room.

"Kiara," Ralph calls out from far away.

All of my energy is on the fire in the center of the room. It's consuming every bit of me.

"Kiara?"

I think I hear Thane's voice. Thoughts of him entering another story, unaided rush me. He's destroying stories, I'm destroying stories. I keep my eyes glued to the fireball, but I see the burning village instead. I see the half-burned, half-beaten woman who pleaded with me to save her child. Tears threaten my vision.

Flames start pouring out of the raging beast. But I can't stop it.

I start panting, but my thoughts continue to wander to the past few days. A rumbling howl grows from the center of the room. Fire is starting to scatter around the room.

"What are you doing?" Ralph shouts as he runs toward me.

I collapse to my knees. I can't control the flames. The fireball begins swirling, testing the failing restraints my power had on it.

Ralph pulls me out from near the center of the room and pushes me against the wall as the fireball bursts, spewing flames everywhere. He throws himself on top of me, fire raining down all around us.

His face contorts in pain as flames land near us. The face of the burned woman from the village appears in front of me. Tears fall from my eyes as something deep inside me registers what is happening.

Soon, the fireball in the center of the room runs out of energy and falls to the ground, starting a large bonfire.

Ralph slumps to the ground. I reach out for him, collapsing with him. I still can't register what happened.

Shouts come down the hall and some people run into the room, gasping at the fires around the room. Someone sees us against the wall, and calls for help.

Ralph is panting and is clearly struggling to breathe.

"We're done for tonight," Ralph pants as someone grabs him, shouting for a medic.

Another cloaked figure pulls me up and starts asking me questions. I continue to stare at Ralph as people start removing the remnants of his shirt, examining the burns.

The person assisting me sees I'm ok and guides me towards the exit.

I wander toward my room as others run for the training room, hands with buckets of water and arms full of other supplies.

I reach my room and close the door, avoiding the oil lamp. I don't want to ask for a shimmer stone either. I remain in front of my door, staring at the darkness in front of me.

What am I doing?

〜💧〜

I must've passed out at some point because I wake up on the floor of my room. I didn't even move from my spot by the door before collapsing. I push myself up, numb to everything.

What have I done? If I was obeying Thane like I should be, I wouldn't be so tired, and Ralph wouldn't be…Tears roll down my face. I pull my limbs in, trying to find some security in the darkness.

But I only feel the coldness of my heart. Memories of the fireball and Ralph's face burn my vision. Why did he do that? Why did I do that? I excel at everything, so why now?

My mind goes blank as I cry in the dark.

What do I do now? It'd be so much easier to just go back and help Thane, blindly doing my job. But why won't my heart agree to it? I cry harder.

Stupid heart, why won't you listen to me? This pain won't happen when everyone is bowing down to Thane. No one will deviate. Blind ignorance, blind obedience, this is what we want.

I push myself up and wipe my face off. I can't let anyone see my tears. I brush my hair and pull my hood back up. Let's see what I can do to help Thane.

I open the door, head held high, and march off down the hall. It's time to fulfill our dreams. Two guards are stationed outside of Thane's study. They nod to me as I open the doors.

The doors shut behind me as I look at the mirror. An image plays on it, but Thane isn't here watching.

But, if the guards are outside, Thane should be in here. I walk towards the mirror and examine the scene.

A cloaked figure is standing with a group of shirtless, tanned boys, all a little younger than me. They approach a man in front of a pen of…lions? The tallest boy, lean with angled features, looks toward the cloaked figure. Thane.

Thane nods at the boy and the boy pulls out a dagger, a wicked smile on his face. He approaches the man, talking and smiling, and then stabs the man in the gut.

I gasp, as the boy yanks the dagger out. The man drops to his knees and the boy grabs the man's head from behind and…I steel myself…he pulls the blade across the man's throat, blood sputtering everywhere. He then shoves the man away and laughs as he falls to the ground.

A biting chill creeps over my extremities as the group continues laughing. They open the cage and lift the dead man in. Something sparkles for a second and the boys toss the man into the lion pen.

I turn away and walk back towards the doors. What is Thane doing? He permitted those boys to kill the man.

"Just check on Thane and leave," I breathe and mutter to myself.

"What was that, Kiara?" I hear a vortex closing and I turn around to a curious Thane.

"Hello, Thane," I respond, my nerves instantly chilled. "I just came to check on you and..." I hesitate. I never just come to check on Thane. I should tell him what happened. I take a deep breath. "Ralph is in the infirmary, it's my fault," I fight back tears. "I-I-I lost control of the fire."

Thane's brows rise. "Are you alright?"

I look up in shock. "I am fine, but-"

"Then, that's all that matters," he smiles.

I'm numb from head to toe. How could he say that? After me, Ralph is one of the most important people in this compound. Thane eyes me, waiting for a response.

I nod. "Yes," I say. I turn and head for the door. "Welcome back," I say over my shoulder.

I close the door behind me and take off down the hall. My mind is going a mile a minute. Thank God I've made a decision, though. I will help Ulterra regain magic. And the next step is to help the hero of the story Thane was just in.

Based on their clothes, and the scenery, they had to be in a desert.

But where? I've read a wide variety of books spanning across multiple deserts. Those clothes, though. And the style, the cuffs around the boys' wrists. Oh, what is that book called? Something takes flight. Uggh. I should have the book somewhere in my room.

I open the door and reach for the oil lamp. My hand freezes, remembering what happened last time I used fire. I turn and dig through a drawer by the door and find a shimmer stone lamp. It's small, but it'll have to do.

I walk over to my small desk, papers and other study items are scattered about the top. I riffle through the books and notes. I know I recently wrote down the title.

Hmmmm, *Night Hunter*, no, that's a historical fiction with monsters. This one feels more like a different land. It lacks magic, it….aha! Yes, *An Eagle Takes Flight*, a story about a boy named Asar. He is working to become a full-fledged priest. He has to overcome personal trials, both from his rivals and his own temperament, to succeed. Another one of the books Thane clams to be all important and so I must read it countless times.

I put the notes and the lamp down and go to lock my door, shoving a trunk in front of it. I can't let anyone barge in on me while I'm gone.

I've got to save Asar from those murderous boys. I take a deep breath.

Here goes nothing.

〰◆〰

I step out onto a busy street. The sun blazes down on this shadow-less town. Without a place to hide, this sweltering heat is going to kill me. I tug at the front of my cloak. Every inch of me is fidgety, crying for me to rip the thing off. But I can't. I can't let anyone see me. Plus, any hint that I got a tan,

55

or more likely, sunburn, from somewhere will lead to a lot of questions.

"Hey, watch it!" a woman shouts as a kid's wail rises above the crowd. "You terrible boys!"

More shouts of anger and surprise erupt from the street dwellers.

I scan the area and see a nearby alleyway. It's better than nothing. While everyone is distracted by the incoming circus, I run and hide.

I stop halfway down the alley and stand near a wall. I know I'm terribly conspicuous, but not many people should be looking down here right now. I look back the way I came, waiting for the commotion to pass.

My pulse races. I shouldn't be interfering, but I fear Thane already ruined the normal course of this story. I need to give Asar some sort of edge, but how?

Movement catches my eye as the boys turn and start running down the alley. Impossible! They weren't supposed to come down here. I examine them, trying to tell how best to interfere. In the lead boy's white-knuckled grip are a few ruffled feathers. His eyes dart around, scanning the area, and occasionally casts a look over his shoulder. So, they are thieves.

I push off the wall and stand in the boys' path.

"Hey, move it," the lead boy shouts.

I summon the wind, using the surrounding buildings to knock them unconscious. Probably shouldn't have been too violent with them, but I panicked.

When I am sure the boys aren't getting back up anytime soon, I step toward the boy holding the feathers and pluck them from his hand.

I straighten and movement catches my eye again.

I gasp.

That idiot boy is standing in front of me. He's terribly pale in comparison to the boys on the ground, but that doesn't stop him from wearing the linen skirt. His stormy hair shines lavender in the light, some of the bangs covering his right eye and his bare chest expands with each breath he is trying to catch.

I take half a step back, my mind running through all the possibilities. An icy chill creeps in as panic overcomes me. I'm such an idiot! He is the last person who was supposed to see me here. Fight or flight instincts kick in, and I decide to book it. A cart blocks the route behind me, so I start running towards him. If I'm lucky, he'll still be stunned.

Feathers in hand, I leap over a few unconscious boys. I pass the boy and keep running, but the boy's reflexes are too fast for me.

He turns and grabs the sleeve of my cloak. The motion tugs my hood down. I turn in response, looking into his face with shock. His deep grey eyes are wide in awe.

Dammit.

I let go of the feathers in my hand as I stare at him. An icy tornado rages in my chest.

I rip my sleeve out of his grip and turn, summoning a vortex. I've got to get out of here. I sprint through the vortex as it closes and I keep running.

The shimmer stone lamp is the only light signaling I'm back in my room. I groan in frustration and kick the trunk in front of the door.

That idiot! I could have taken care of everything! Why did he have to get in the way? I scream and throw *An Eagle Takes Flight* across the room. It thumps into the wall, and lands with a thud.

Idiot!

〰🌢〰

Someone knocks on my door long after I calmed down, though the thought of that idiot's shocked face prickles my skin like icicles. I sit up on my bed, groggy from a fitful sleep.

"Kiara, Thane wants to see you in his study," Ralph calls out.

I jump out of bed at the sound of his voice and run for the door.

Trunk aside, I tear the door open and see a bandaged Ralph staring at me with tired eyes. My smile fades as I examine just how bad Ralph is. His cloak is open and his chest is wrapped in bandages. His head has a few bandages wrapped around it, and from the looks of it, his hands are burned and bandaged as well. He takes a step back and starts walking in the direction of Thane's study. I shut my door behind me and follow after him.

HQ is dead silent, telling me it must be the middle of the night. What could Thane possibly be doing? Of course, he could have sent everyone out on a mission. But then the question still stands: what could Thane be doing?

We walk to Thane's study without a word, passing shimmer stone lights as we go. Someone replaced the torches in the halls between my room and Thane's study. I am relieved, but still feel horribly guilty. It's because of me – I can't control fire. It's because of me that Ralph looks like this. I fumble through possible things to say to him. I'm sorry just isn't going to cut it.

Before I come up with anything of importance to say, we reach the study doors.

"Go on in, he's waiting for you," Ralph says. His eyes don't show disdain or regret. But they don't show pleasure either. He has to know I feel terrible. I bite my lip and look down.

A padded hand rests on my shoulder. "Just go in," Ralph says. I look back at him and I can swear I see a trace of something. Not care, or concern, but something that tells me he doesn't blame me for the accident.

I swallow and nod. One problem down, another one to face. I open the polished wood doors and enter the chamber.

Thane is, once again, standing and staring at the mirror. This mirror obsession is going to be the end of him. Once the doors are closed, I approach him.

The atmosphere in here is as awkward as a still candle flame.

"Would you look at this?" Thane asks without turning to me. He knows I'm already looking.

The scene is outside a spacious, open building, a walkway of pristine columns leading to the entrance. Next to the building, there is a lake, with little foliage surrounding it. The stars of the night sky reflect in the semi-still water. Ripples recede from a figure, kneeled down near the edge of the water.

The figure is hunched over, not moving a muscle. Suddenly, the figure swats at the water, once again disturbing the serene night. The mirror pans in a little closer, in time to show the man throw his head back in what I imagine is a heart-wrenching scream. He holds it and collapses to the ground, not moving again. It's the idiot boy.

"What happened?" I ask.

"Our little hero boy just killed Uthman," Thane says, a smile snaking around his face.

My heart stops. "He killed someone?" I ask in disbelief.

"Yes, it seems the boy isn't as pure as that witch thinks."

"But what happened?" I'm still confused by what this means. Why is this so important for Thane to show me?

"Things got out of control and the little hero had to dirty his hands," Thane's wicked smile grows. "Uthman failed securing some of the ritual items, so he had to resort to other measures."

I choke. *Failed securing some of the ritual items*? The feathers…

I stare at the figure passed out beside the lake. He had to kill someone because I intervened. Tears well in my eyes, but I blink them away.

"You don't seem too upset," I say.

"Oh, I am, but this did two things for me," Thane looks at me, a knowing look in his eyes.

I stare at him, waiting for his answer. I've learned long ago not to play guessing games with Thane. His answers are either painfully obvious or deeply convoluted.

"One, the boy took care of Uthman for me, meaning I don't need to deal with him myself. Two, it showed me the darkness I knew the boy had in him. I was wondering when he would embrace it."

Thane is always far too vague. I swear he knows things about me, about this boy, about everything, before they happen. He never acknowledges it, but he knows something more than he is letting on.

I nod and look back at the scene. Some figures step out into the night and walk towards the boy. A dog-like creature stops them and herds them back to the building before they disturb him.

Frosty vines wrap around my heart, stopping it from its rampage. It's time I got back on track. It's time I continue with my original plan: keep my head down, follow Thane diligently, and accept the outcomes. The world's magic isn't my responsibility. I need to find my brother, that's all that matters. But my heart still holds onto the thought of magic in the world. Perhaps, with magic, I will have an easier time finding Ewan. Regardless, Thane really wants a reaction from me.

I take a sharp breath in, and slowly exhale. "He won't be so successful next time."

Thane turns to me, but I don't look at him. I know his golden eyes are dancing in delight.

I growl. A major meeting was called, and I wasn't invited.

What will people think when Thane's right hand isn't there at the meeting? And I need to keep an eye on his movements until I make my decision – to help him or stop him.

I shake my head. It'll be hard to tell Thane that I think we've been going about all of this "Era of Peace and Happiness" the wrong way. I take a back route to the Assembly hall. The hallway isn't ornate like the main one leading to the meeting room, but the shimmer stones are bright enough to tell no one is lurking in the shadows. Only Thane, myself, and Ralph are allowed to use this hallway to the meeting room anyway. It's like a secret passage for royalty.

I'm not a princess though, despite being royally pissed. Sure, I've been going behind his back, but he has no reason to keep me in the dark. I stop my stomping and creep toward the curtain and nudge it aside so I can peek out.

"The nest is located under the Steline Mountains, about three days from here. Prepare yourselves well, for dragons are tough to beat." He paces. "Your goal is the eggs though, not the dragon. If you can keep it distracted, then more of you will make it out." He stops to look at the hooded faces. "Time is of the essence. You are dismissed," Thane commands.

Cloaked figures scramble to get out of the assembly hall. He sighs and rests his cheek on his hand, watching the team disappear.

"Tell me, Gareth, will all of this work?"

Gareth steps out of the shadows. "It should. Dragon eggs are pure magic sir, and our scouts have reported that these eggs were laid not too long ago. The quartz we gathered earlier will store the energy, but you'll have to carry a piece with you."

"Very well, that's no problem," Thane says.

"Well, there is a problem," Gareth says.

Thane shifts and looks at him, not seeming to be bothered by Gareth's tone.

"We will have to be careful and mediate your use of these items. I know you have been using the quartz and the magic stored in them, but too much extra magic in such a short amount of time will have adverse effects."

Adverse effects? Why has he been using quartz mediators without my knowledge? I clench my fists to stop my trembling. He shouldn't be doing this without my help, but he is.

"What adverse effects, Gareth?"

"The worst one is magic toxicosis. If you use too much outside magic, it will consume you. It poisons your blood and your mind. It affects everyone differently, but the end is the same for everyone. You lose yourself, your humanity, and eventually, if you are lucky, you will die."

Gareth's words pierce my heart. I can't let Thane kill himself! Not like this. I bite back a growl. Why can't he talk to me about this?

"Is that all?" Thane asks, putting his chin back on his palm.

"But, sir!"

"Is that all?" Thane repeats.

"Yes," Gareth says, bowing his head.

Chapter 8

"Now, earth is going to be tough to manipulate. It's stoic, set in its ways. So, I think we should work with water next. I have a feeling she will have an affinity for it," Gareth comments.

The carriage hits a bump in the road, jarring me from my vacant stare at the rolling landscape. I rest my chin on my hand again, refocusing out the window. Ralph coughs in attempts to get my attention. I don't care what I do next. I just don't want to touch fire. Gareth clears his throat and I shoot him a look. It's not like I have a say in any of this, it's all Thane's choice anyway.

Ralph sighs. "I think water would be a good element to switch to. Have you come up with a new plan?"

"I have," Gareth nods, "we will learn about the properties of the elements before moving to use them. I think if she were to have a better understanding of each element, then she will have an easier time controlling them."

I roll my eyes and pull myself away from the conversation and focus on the trip. Thane has scheduled an outing for us to head back to Lummava. I'm thrilled to meet with Heinz again, especially since I'm running low on tea herbs. I have been making double batches lately, giving half to Ralph in place of an apology. He's not much of a tea drinker, but the healers have said he's been doing better since he's started drinking it. Ralph's not superstitious, but I have a feeling he won't stop drinking it until he has a clean bill of health.

"So, what does Thane have planned anyway?" I ask, finally ready to join the conversation. "And why are so few of us going?"

"We are going on a retrieval mission in Lummava. Slipping in with fewer numbers will...?" Gareth trails off with a raised brow.

I sigh. "Slipping in with fewer numbers will not only keep our intent a secret, but will allow us to leave with fewer casualties, to both sides – which is why Thane summoned his stealth squad last week. They've been doing recon on whatever we're supposed to be retrieving. But, why does Thane insist on having his own carriage?"

"He's taking a different route," Ralph says. He crosses his arms and looks out his window. Two fancy carriages, each signifying an important Gemini member is inside. If we are taking the direct route to Lummava, then Thane…

"No. He. Didn't," I say.

Ralph glances at me and then back out the window, his jaw clenched. Gareth looks at me and nods.

"A decoy?" I shout. "He's using us as a decoy!" This has to be punishment for something. He never uses me, *me*, as a decoy. That self-righteous…I growl.

"Relax, Kiara," Gareth says. I glare at him. "That's why we're here. Thane is traveling alone."

I scrunch my upper lip in disgust. "That makes us more of a target."

Gareth stares at me. He didn't want me adding things together. Too bad for him, I like math.

I throw myself back in my seat and cross my arms in a huff. "Whatever." We'll be in Lummava soon, and a visit with Heinz will make things better.

Chapter 9

Some kids run by laughing and shouting. I watch them go, weaving in and out of the crowds of people. It's a cool day, but the sun is shining, a rare sight in fall. It's a great day for a festival.

"This is a good spot."

Heinz sits down at the edge of the fountain in the middle of Lummava's very busy plaza. I slink back as a family of kitsune passes by. Today must be a festival of some sort. Vendors, musicians, actors, and a million other beings from across the land are crying out to each other. I scurry into the fray to find Heinz.

I sit down next to the old man. As soon as I could shake Ralph and Gareth, I ran to Heinz's herb shop. He set me up with a ton of herbs, especially after I told him about Ralph's injuries. Well, I left out the details that it was my fault. I stare at my hands.

"So, Kiara, how have you been?" Heinz's eyes twinkle.

"I've been better," I sigh. I notice the old man's concern and quickly add, "I'm just positively exhausted. I've been training a lot more, and my tutor has dumped even more work on me, not to mention the work the group has me doing, and..."

"...and?"

"And it's exhausting work," I finish. I can't tell him about my traitorous activities. I look behind me at the water in the fountain. It ripples with the falling water from the phoenix statue in the center. I smirk. A phoenix immersed in water, what idiot thought that was a good idea?

I dip my fingers in the water and drag them along, letting the coolness of the water sink in. As I lift my fingers out of the water, droplets follow, hovering in the air. I smile fondly. I have always loved water. Not the drink, but the element. It's such an impressive force. It is harsh and angry, carving its own path, but it can be gentle and nurturing, healing those who have been hurt in the heat of battle. I switch my focus back to Heinz, listening to the droplets fall back into the water.

"You seem even less happy than the last time I saw you. Of course, the light is better out here," Heinz jokes.

I laugh. "Heinz, you really need to invest in some shimmer stones."

"You kids and your new toys," Heinz shakes his head.

I laugh harder. "Heinz! Shimmer stones are as old as the planet!"

He laughs. "I know, I know, I just wanted to see a smile on your face."

I flush a little at the thought.

"Kiara," his face gets serious, "what is really going on? This group of yours seems to make you upset."

I sigh. If I can't tell Heinz, I'll never be able to tell anyone about it. But do I really want to do that? What if it gets him in trouble? I tuck my hair behind my ear.

"Heinz, that village…" I say, voice trembling.

"The one near Ephemeral Mine?" I nod. "What about it?"

I look ahead and take a deep breath. "Heinz, I was there. Those people, all they wanted was to enjoy their lives. They were good people. They…suffered because they wouldn't bow to Thane." I say what he did to them. I was useless. I was heartless, *am* heartless. I heard their screams for help as their houses burned down around them, and yet I did nothing.

"I watched as a woman reached out for me. She was beaten beyond recognition. I just stared at her…" my eyes tear and I shake my head feverishly. "He speaks of acceptance, but kills all in his way. He dreams of equality, but looks down on those who are different from him. I…just…" My shoulders slump.

I can't do this anymore. But I have to. I think about everything that goes wrong when I go against Thane's plans. Ralph is still in bandages and he is expected to perform all his duties still.

"True equality can never be achieved," Heinz says looking wistful. "In rights? Absolutely. In every other sense? Impossible. We are all born different, male and female, human and elf, ogre and goblin, king and peasant, you and me. It's these differences that make this crazy thing called life worth living.

"These differences help us progress and create new and beautiful things. Sure, we can be destructive and hateful. We can't seem to bridge the gap between what makes me, me, and you, you. Besides taking the time to talk over some good tea, I can't say what we should do to stop people from hurting each other. But do you know what I do?" I shake my head. "I always make sure I'm not in such a hurry that I can't help someone in need."

I open my mouth, but Heinz stops me.

"I'm an old man. I don't have all the answers. You say you like their ideals, but hate their methods. Perhaps, you should set out on your own path, show them there is another way. I get the feeling you might have started already."

My cheeks heat with color. He knows. He knows just by looking at me that I have been working against Thane and the others.

"There is a light in you, I've seen it," he continues. "People are attracted to it and follow you. You have the light, the heart, and the brains, now let the world see it." Heinz laughs and winks.

I turn away from him. These are the kindest words I have ever heard. And he said them about me. Despite the monster I am, he believes in me. I suddenly become very self-aware. Even with this cloak, I feel a chill wash over me. I feel overly exposed. I look up and see, between people passing back and forth, the idiot boy staring at me.

His grey eyes are questioning, observing everything that has been going on here. I glare at him. How dare he listen in on our conversation! Yes, we are out in public, but there are so many people walking around that I couldn't imagine anyone else bothering to listen to an old man and a foolish girl.

Then behind him, Ralph fades into sight. He stares at me, his eyes saying it's time. He then melts back into the crowd. I look back at the boy, who is still staring at me with that stupid look of his.

"Heinz, I'm sorry, but I have somewhere I need to be." I nod at the man who waves, I put my hood back up, and join the crowd. I've got to find out where Ralph is headed, soon.

I swallow at the thought of Ralph also listening in on our conversation. He'll tell Thane. He has every right to turn me in. I bite my lip. I can't show weakness now.

I head toward the edge of the plaza and find Ralph and Gareth near one of the shops. Everyone here is distracted by the festivities, so they won't pay any mind to three hooded figures.

"Is it time?" I ask as I join the pair.

"Yes, it's been time. I had a hell of a time finding you," Ralph growls.

"I'm sorry. I was getting some of that tea you like so much," I say.

He growls again. "Looked more like a tea party."

"That old man, he just loves to talk. I was just being nice," I say.

I know that didn't convince either of them, but they let it go.

"This way," Gareth says, "to the manor on the hill."

We reach a wrought iron fence in front of one of the most stunning buildings I have ever seen. The manor is enchanting with its ivy-covered walls. The windows remain unlit, but that is expected for such a glorious day. The curtains are closed though, telling me no one is using the rooms, or housekeeping has been shirking their duties.

Inside the fence is a lovely courtyard, lush with plants. That can't be right. A lot of the trees have started losing their leaves, but the trees in the courtyard are still green, like it's mid-spring. The trees aren't even evergreens, they should've lost their leaves!

This is the first clue that we are retrieving something magical.

"Glad to see you all," Thane finally says.

"Is this all of us?" Ralph asks, scanning the area for movement.

"Not quite. I have the stealth squad in position. They will be entering before us, from all sides. Then we will go in after them."

"Sir, pardon my questioning, but why am I here?" Gareth asks.

"I need you here to identify a very important book for me."

Gareth looks surprised. "What book might that be?"

"*A Fighting Chance*," Thane answers, looking at the manor behind him. "The original version," he adds, turning back to Gareth.

"A first edition? But those have long since disappeared from Maailma, probably all of Ulterra."

I look at Gareth, examining his expression. I've never read the book. I actually don't know much about it except that it's a love story. I may secretly enjoy a good love story; I prefer my books to have more meat to them.

"That is precisely why we need to grab this one," Thane smiles at me.

If my memory serves me, original versions of stories are where the real magic lies, not saying that retellings lack magic. It's just the original seems to hold the magic in its purest form. In order for any of us to get into the story, we need to have knowledge of the story, at least the part where we want to enter.

"What's in *A Fighting Chance*?" I ask. I'm not really sure I want to enter a love story.

"The strongest magic," Thane smiles. "Now, if that's all of the questions, it's time."

I take a deep breath. Let's do this.

Thane waves an arm and shadows from trees and other fixtures jump out and swarm the manor. A group of three break through the front doors, rushing in with the blink of an eye.

Thane nods to Ralph, who pushes open the wrought iron fence, and he leads the way to the manor. Gareth and I flank Thane, searching for signs of an activating security. Houses this grand tend to have their own mini-armies. But this place seems oddly unguarded. This could be thanks to the stealth squad, but a whisper in the back of my mind says I'm wrong.

Stepping into the courtyard is an odd sensation. It tingles with familiarity, with comfort. Maybe Thane and I visited this place years ago. We did a lot of traveling when I was younger. We charge through the courtyard and march into the manor.

The inside gives me a dizzying sensation. Not enough to throw off my balance, but enough to confuse my thoughts. I follow behind Thane, taking in the details of the hallway.

Polished wood floors and walls scream money. The portraits that line the way are beautifully done. They seem to be painted by the same artist. I catch a name on one of the plaques under a painting, as we walk by.

An Eagle Takes Flight? That was the last book the idiot boy was in. My temper pierces through the dizziness.

Thane marches to the end of the hall and into a grand room. Members of the stealth squad are surrounding two downed figures. They are still moving, but they know they are grossly outnumbered.

My eyes widen when I see the Va'ahn struggling to sit up. He's been beaten something fierce, just like the woman next to him.

"Well, hello there my dear Clara," Thane says, clasping his hands behind his back.

The stealth squad shifts out of his way, keeping an eye on the captives. Gareth and I follow behind him.

Despite the scrapes, cuts, and bruises, I can tell that Clara is positively beautiful. She has, *had*, perfect porcelain skin, her hair is so fair with the tint of pink in it. Around the back of her neck are golden spikes, looking like rays of sun. I look at her eyes and I'm taken back. She's young, not more than five years older than me, but her face! Through the scrapes I can see her skin is wrinkling and sagging. There is something terribly off about her. It's like she's sick.

"Thane," she seethes. I can feel the venom when she speaks.

Thane squats down next to her and puts his fingers under her chin, forcing her to look at him.

He smiles an equally venomous smile. "Long time, no see."

She looks at him in surprise and confusion, the same things I feel.

He stands back up and strolls over to a nearby table. He picks up the book laying there and flips through it.

"Ah, yes, you can almost *feel* the magic coming out of this book." He snaps it shut.

"Thane, don't you dare," she puffs.

"Why Clara, when did you get your bite back?" Thane strolls around, examining the victims.

Clara gets up to lunge at Thane. Before I can react, one of the stealth squad members hits her, knocking back on her legs. A simple analysis of her says she shouldn't be beaten this easily. My deduction of her must be correct. I grimace.

Thane strolls over to Gareth and hands him the book. "Is this it?"

Gareth begins a thorough examination of the text. He studies the cover and flips through the pages, searching for specific pages. He carefully closes the book and looks at Thane. "It is."

An eerie smile grows on Thane's face. "My, my, keeping such a powerful book to yourself. That's very selfish of you, Clara."

"It's not for you to have," Clara spits.

"Of course, it isn't. I'm just going to give it a better home." Thane stalks around the room examining everything in it. He strolls by the book wall, running his finger along the spines. He chooses one at random and pulls it out.

"Stop it, Thane. You will never win this battle." Clara cries. My heart ices over. Nothing disgusts me more than a weak female.

Thane walks back over to her, book still in hand. He looks at her, feigning care and love.

Her eyes are wide and darting left and right, fear has taken hold of her. Thane smirks and tears the book in half. The wind is knocked out of me. My lungs scream for air, but I can't move. Tears start flowing out of Clara's eyes, an expression of the pain I'm feeling.

"You know what to do," Thane says. He stands and signals for Ralph, Gareth, and me to follow him out of the manor.

I hear screams of agony as things are tossed, ripped, and thrown around the room. Then, another thud and the screams stop. I cringe and keep walking. I follow Thane out of the manor and down the winding path, back towards town.

A man jumps out in front of Thane. I brace myself for a fight, but I'm the only one who is tense. Thane and the man have a brief conversation.

"Found him, sir," the man says.

"Great! Things are certainly looking up today," Thane says.

"What should we do about him?" the man asks, not showing a hint of the same sentiment Thane expressed.

"Do what you will. Just make sure he doesn't speak against me again."

The man nods and disappears again. My nerves are getting to me. For some reason, I feel Heinz is in serious trouble.

"What a lovely day, isn't it?" Thane asks as he stretches.

I look at the sky. Lovely isn't the word I'd use.

Chapter 10

"Kiara, Thane has left instructions for you," a member says. He hands me the note and leaves. I shut the door behind him, staring at the folded note in my hand.

Thane usually briefs me on situations himself. I open the note and see Thane's meticulous handwriting scrawled on the paper.

Gone to do some work, trying to stop this problem as soon as I can.

I need you to take care of something for me.

There is a little nuisance of a character running around in A Lady's Resolve.

I believe she might be key in your brother's disappearance.

You'll find her on page 1█7 of the text Gareth gave you.

Dispatch her at once.

-Thane

There is a smudge on the page number. I stare at it. It's strange for Thane to make such a mistake when he is so annoyingly meticulous with everything. Maybe he was in a hurry.

I stare at my desk, the shimmer stone lamp lighting the small space. My brother? How can a character in *A Lady's Resolve* be involved with my brother's disappearance? Emotions wash over me like the ocean mid-storm. My brother! I can't believe it's a clue in my brother's disappearance.

Nuisance of a character? Maybe this person is one of those story walkers Gareth told me about. Let's see if I can remember correctly. Sometimes people get caught in stories, a thin gap in space time or a strong affinity to the story…or something like that. Maybe this person is from our world and is responsible for my brother's disappearance.

My blood boils. Why couldn't Thane ask me himself? He knows that Gareth has switched focus from the world's oldest stories, to the elements. The page number is here, but I don't know in what context I'm going to find everything. I don't have time to read up to and through page 107.

I pace back and forth when there is a knock on my door. I open the door, expecting Thane to apologize and explain himself. What, or who, I find is Ralph. His arms are crossed and he is giving me an unreadable expression. His muscular build, mixed with his bandages, provide a terrifying image.

He hands me an envelope. "Here," he grunts. He leaves without another word.

I shut the door again, and stare at the envelope. Another note? So soon?

My name is written across the front in Thane's script. I sigh. Maybe this is an apology.

Kiara,

I'm sorry I couldn't brief you myself-

Well, that's an apology…

Something came up of the upmost importance. As time is of the essence if we want to succeed, I have been forced to take matters into my own hand. By the time you are done with your session with Gareth, I'll be gone on my mission. I have left an assignment for you with a member of the stealth squad. Please see Ralph if you don't receive it soon.

I am depending on you, Kiara. You are like a sister to me and I wish to keep you safe. That is why I'm doing this. Please understand. I'll make this up to you when I return. Though I believe the mission will be an adequate start.

With all my heart,

Thane

Tears well as I choke back a sob. He's never said such things to me. He's always been like an older brother to me. I bite my lip.

But he's been killing people. He's been so angry and distant lately. His methods are atrocious, they're unforgiveable. I can't stand it. But…

I look back at his note. He's always been there for me. He's doing this for us, for everyone who has been hurt. He stayed up nights with me when I was scared. He bandaged my cuts and scrapes, and he would tell me the most fantastic bedtime stories.

I sway and plop down on my bed. Warring emotions fight through my thoughts. Do I betray the man who is like a brother to me? The man who will help me *find* my brother…or do I do as Heinz says and create my own path?

The pressure to decide has me frozen. I take a deep breath.

"Let's handle this logically," I murmur into the silence.

There is always time to forge my own path. And Thane might just take some convincing, nothing else. We could sit down and formulate a plan going forward. He doesn't know how I feel. If he is doing this for us, maybe he thinks I'm ok with the "demon be damned" attitude.

Note two, every time I've gone against him, it hasn't ended well. This would mean ignoring his orders would have unintended consequences, maybe on him. Ralph has been hurt, the idiot boy had to kill, someone was killed. What if, I gulp, dispatching this person is the only way to prevent further harm to others? It still doesn't sit right, but Thane has everyone's best interests at heart. Well, at least the interests of Gemini members…

I stand up. Yes, this is fine. It's just a storybook character. I'm not actually hurting anyone. Then, once Thane and I are done with our missions, we can sit down, perhaps over some of Heinz's tea blend, and discuss my new ideas.

I smile, a fool's smile, but I don't care. This is going to work. I toss the note on my bed and rifle through the book stack on my desk. *A Lady's Resolve*, there it is.

I flip through the pages and read page 106 to the end of 107. Ok, so Sophia, who sounds like the protagonist, is away to check on evidence, and her maid is busying herself around the house. The maid must be my target. I swallow.

Just a character.

Chapter 11

I stare in front of me, my vision completely blurred. I take a few paces back, not moving my gaze. My heart pounds, like hail on a cottage roof. Tears sting my eyes. I blink them away, my vision clearing momentarily. I drop something, not sure what it was. I don't remember much.

I clearly recall opening a vortex. When I went through, I found myself inside a house or manor of some sort. I remember muddling through some stray thoughts, trying to rein them in before I…I what? Now, I'm frozen, pulse racing so fast I can hear it in my ears. Everything in between is a complete blur.

I whip my head toward the front door. Laughter and voices sound over my pulse. Someone is coming. Ice water runs through my veins, urging my body to move. My animalistic instincts take over and I start panicking.

I've got to get out of here. I turn and run. I push through a door as I hear the door open and the voices enter the house. Where do I go? What do I do? Why do I need to run? A scream sounds from the front of the house, piercing through my clouded thoughts.

I-I-I…

I exit the kitchen. I hear footsteps coming after me. I run faster. I need to get out of here. I need to go. I need air. I can't breathe. I bolt through ornately decorated rooms and into a study. The sight of the neatly organized desk and the smell of leather books calm my nerves enough for me to make a quick decision. I run to the window and throw it open.

The night air greets my face as I lean out. This will have to do. I tumble out the window, somersaulting on the ground. I get up and survey the yard. No one is out here, but I can't see a way for me to escape. I run to the side of the house.

I hear a groan as someone else lands outside the window. Tears sting my eyes. It wasn't me. I couldn't have. I never would have. I keep running, my lungs stinging like thousands of little splinters are piercing them. I can't stop though. They can't catch me.

They-

Something comes swinging at my face. The impact knocks all of my thoughts from my head and I fall. I hear footsteps slow down as they approach me. Then there is some mumbling. Then…darkness.

I'm standing in a dark, empty space. I would say it's a room, but I can't determine where the walls are. I take a few steps forward, and though I know I'm moving, I don't make it anywhere. I take a couple more steps. Movement feels better than standing still. Each step starts sloshing, like I am wading in ankle deep water.

I look down and find dark water covering my brown boots. When did the water get here? I shiver. I keep walking, but the water is rising. I run. I take panicked breaths, not sure where the water ends, where I will be able to find dry land.

The water is mid-thigh now. My cloak drags behind me like a parachute, impeding my progress. I take a few deep breaths to calm my nerves and to stop the tears from coming. What did I do? How did I get here? Something tells me I belong here, that somehow, I deserve what's coming. I look around as I scream for help, but no sound comes out of my mouth.

I stop moving and focus on my breaths. My mind refuses to stop its torrent of images and thoughts. They speed by, each one making less sense then the last. Something is wrong, something is-

There. I saw movement. The form leaps around on the water but doesn't make a single splashing sound. It's as if the creature is above the water, as if it doesn't obey the natural laws. My normal fight or flight instincts stay dormant. I stare at the creature. It hops from place to place, slowly making its way toward me.

The water is at my shoulders. I reach a hand out for the creature. I need it to save me. I tilt my head back to prevent the water from covering my nose. I glance back at the creature, then ice cold water rains down on my face.

I gasp and gulp for air. I try to wipe the droplets off my face, but my arms don't move. I try again with more force and feel the binds keeping them down. I shake my head, keenly aware there are eyes on me. Once I am satisfied that I won't get any water in my eyes, I open them and see the idiot boy, arms crossed, glaring at me.

His anger clashes with my own smoldering hatred for him. I glare at him. I know exactly where I am, I know what I've done, and I know I want out. I clench my jaw and ready myself for what is either going to be a beating or an interrogation, or both.

"Good, you're awake," he says. "We are going to ask you questions and you are going to cooperate." I laugh, it's sounds strained, but it's genuine.

I can't believe this idiot. The last time I saw him he was bawling his eyes out, now he's trying to act like some tough detective.

"Like that is going to happen." I roll my eyes. His anger flares. Oh yes, this will be fun.

"Oh, I think it will." I match his glare, smugness coming over me. Something about this little moment feels familiar, but I shove the thought down. I'm out for blood, I can't let other emotions sway me. I think about some conversations I had with Thane.

"What are you going to do if I don't? You couldn't kill a lion; do think you can hurt a defenseless girl?" I bat my eyelashes, giving him sweet and innocent.

That really gets to him.

"Just don't try me," he finally says. Oh, he's definitely struggling to keep himself in line. I smirk.

"What is your name?" one of the elf girls asks.

"Wouldn't you like to know?" I roll my head to look at her.

This is the first time I have seen either elf girl this close up. They are wearing makeup, but after our little cat and mouse chase, one of her pointed ears are sticking out of her partial up do. She's wearing makeup, and as I'm embarrassed to admit, a gorgeous dress and jewelry to match. I'd love to have an occasion to wear a dress at least half as nice as hers. Maybe Thane will throw a party after all of this is over. He always tells me that once he succeeds, I can take the title of Princess, and princesses get to wear dresses if it pleases them. Though I would loathe to wear a dress every day.

"Tell us your name," the idiot boy seethes stepping forward.

We glare at each other, willing the other to give up. Something flashes in my memory again, a feeling of remembrance stirs, and then quickly fades. This makes me lose the intensity of my gaze and I turn away and sigh. We are getting nowhere and I need to find a way out.

"Kiara." I clench my teeth.

"That's a start," he says, pulling away from me. He reeks of smugness.

I want to punch him.

"Are you a Shadow Dweller?" the elf by the window asks.

"Yeah, your point?" I ask, rhetorically.

Her dress is equally as elegant as her sister's. I admire it. From my observations, she appears to be the nicer, easier going of the two. Well, three if I count the buffoon. Something feels off about that sentiment. Maybe it's because they are my enemies.

I glance at the boy. Heat radiates off him. He must be a pain to work with. "Where is the Shadow Dweller King? Where is this Thane person who attacked Clara and Tyre?"

These questions tell me quite a bit about the situation. I smile inwardly. They really shouldn't let him do interrogations. Of course, I am worried. With this temper, he's capable of anything, and he's after Thane. If he knew I was there for the attack, he could kill me. I need to warn Thane, but where is he? What I really need is a travel version of Thane's mirror so I can see where he is.

Something hits me like a jolt of lightning. Thane's here, he's in this story. A blizzard of thoughts and emotions blankets my mind, preventing me from seeing straight. I need to get out of here as soon as I can. I close my eyes to calm the storm. This is no time for me to lose my head. I need to focus. I open my mouth and spit out the first thing that comes to mind.

"Oh, he has been closer to you then you think. I know you have seen him." I smirk deviously. Chew on that, pretty boy.

"Why are you destroying the stories? What is your goal?" he asks.

I stare down at my knees, leaning as far over as the restraints will let me. I watch droplets of water roll off my wet hair. Why is Thane destroying stories? Our goal is absolute domination, a world of no will, a world of complete submission. We call it the Era of Peace and Happiness. It's a stupid name, but that's what I called it when I was twelve. Thane used the name, and it stuck.

I feel broken. Twelve-year-old me seems so young and innocent now. I shiver, the cold water slowly drying. I want to clutch onto the distant memory of me discussing an idealist world with Thane. How have we strayed so far from then? My heart shatters. Leaving nothing but a dark hole, cold air blowing right through it.

"Why not?" I say, trying to hide my exasperation. I notice I might have failed, so I try to compensate for it. "Didn't your precious Clara tell you? We want to rule the world. We want to take people's willingness to resist; a subservient population. It's a dream come true." I smile at him, but I don't feel any joy.

I watch a wide array of emotions dance in his eyes. I even briefly think joy and amusement might have shown, though I'm sure I misread it. "Next question," he says.

Someone raps on the door and enters. A girl with golden blonde hair, that puts mine to shame, stumbles in. She would be absolutely stunning if she hadn't been crying. Her rose red dress has dark spots on it, some of it from her tears, others….

"What have you gotten out of her?" Sophia asks coldly. She gives an icy stare to the boy.

The boy examines her, unsure of what to make of her behavior. Though I'm sure, like every other guy, he's afraid of her because she is crying. I shake my head at the thought. It took Ralph a long time to get used to my crying when I was growing up. He's about the same age as Thane, but seems to lack the big brother instincts. I think a lot of his actions actually come from the desire to prevent me from crying. Thane though had to deal with crying the night we met. I had just lost my parents and my…I grind my teeth, forcing the memory down.

"We know her name," he says, "and not much else."

I stare at him. He is keeping our world a secret from her. That tells me enough about her and why she is crying. I take a deep breath to steady myself. I would have to face this sooner or later.

"Are you the one who has been committing these murders?" I feel the venom dripping off her words.

For all the boy's attempts at being intimidating, he fell short. But this girl, she's got it down. I want to feel hatred for her, or something. I quickly glance at the boy to stir some anger in me, but nothing happens. I look back at her. I feel as dead as her…

"Yes and no," I respond.

This doesn't get the reaction I want. Her cold glare is heating up. She's going to blow.

"Answer the question, in detail, who is committing these murders?" she asks again.

Her stillness is frightening. She's a predator waiting for her prey to make the wrong move. Something does stir in me, though it's not the emotion I was looking for.

I want to protect my family. "Like I'd tell y-"

I'm cut off. My face stings before I register the sound of skin hitting skin. My face is sent to the side, my eyes wide. Did she hit me? Then something hits me harder. The weight of what I did. She is a character in a book, but she hit me. I felt it. It stings with all the emotions she is feeling. She is feeling things. She is suffering the loss of a friend. She isn't just some character in a book, she's as real as I am.

"I killed Delma," I say. The reality of the words sinks in.

She didn't see me coming. I entered the story somewhere in the house and snuck up behind the maid. She was humming a tune to herself, proudly going about her work. My thoughts swirled together like a whirlpool, keeping me in the present. I kept telling myself I was doing this for my brother, but would he have wanted this? Thane told me this would be a step toward saving my brother. Did he lie to me? Did he use me? Has he been using me?

"Why? Why Delma? I can't speak for the other women, but Delma was a kind woman and a good friend. Why?" Sophia says. She then breaks down into sobs for her friend.

My heart would wrench to see this, if it was still intact. I stare distantly at her. My gut knots, telling me I definitely was wrong in this. No one says a word as we watch the woman sob on the floor. Cold remorse fills me. Sure, I'm sad for her, but I'm sorry for me. Where did I go wrong? That woman had nothing to do with Ewan, she was in Thane's way, and he used me.

"I was under orders," I whisper. "I...I was fed false information. She wasn't meant to die."

I struggle to breathe. I look at the boy, searching for some sort of understanding. Somewhere deep in his eyes I can see it. I know I'm not imagining this. He feels something besides flaming rage.

I sift through the event that led me here. The note from the one member, the note from Ralph, the text, then I recall something I thought was strange. The first note, the one detailing my mission, there was a smudge on the middle of the page number. It wasn't a zero, it was an eight. I dismissed it as an accident, but I'm sure now, it was supposed to be page 187. That means it should have been closer to the end of the book. Which means...the maid shouldn't have died.

I look at the sobbing woman. She was the one I was supposed to kill.

"Who are you after?" the idiot asks. I look up at him. He has a knack for asking things I am just now realizing.

"Sophia," I answer. I look down at my shaking knees. The cloak is damp, but is drying. I shuffle my feet a little, trying to feel the carpet through my boots.

"What? Why?" he asks. He steps closer to me to urge me to focus on him.

I close my eyes, refusing to do this anymore. I want out. I don't care what I need to do, I'm done. I'm no closer to finding Ewan than the night he went missing. "Her death will guarantee our success." Is that enough of an answer for him?

Sophia howls when she hears this, an expected response. The lighter haired twin escorts the woman out of the room. A low growl is coming from the boy.

"You see what you have done? You have killed countless people for the sake of some stupid plan!" He is fuming.

His words sting like the freezing winter wind. I tense. I must have royally screwed up if this idiot is lecturing me.

"I didn't kill them…" I mumble. He needs to get one thing straight, I'm no monster. I may be heartless, now more than ever, but there is no way I went around killing others. How can he think that? Doesn't he see how much the maid's death is affecting me?

The twin returns to the room. "Sophia says the police will be here soon, they will be taking Delma and Kiara." She looks at me with solemn filled eyes. Not a trace of loathing can be found on her face.

Then her words sink in. I tense again. The billions of pieces of my heart thump in time together. I look around. I need to get out of here. I can't be caught. I need to make this right. I need to find Ewan. The boy notices my panic and my smugness returns. He wants to stop me. He did it once before, but I'm not going to be beaten twice.

"I would like to see them try," I say.

I summon a gentle wind to blow out the oil lamps, and knock the lights out. I then use the wind to slice my bindings. Once they're cut, I shoot out of the chair and away from the center of the room. I hear everyone fumbling around, trying to find a way to light the room. I open a vortex and get the hell out of there.

〜◆〜

In my panic, I didn't focus on where I wanted the vortex to open. I just knew I wanted to go somewhere safe. I blink, nervous for a second that I didn't actually leave the story. I feel around and notice I'm in my bedroom closet. I slump to the ground, giving myself a moment's reprieve. I escaped again. I've been cutting it close lately. I've really got to stop it.

I take a deep breath and open the door. My room is exactly how I left it. I stumble to my bed and fall on it, face first. I roll over and stare at the rocky ceiling of my room. It's faintly illuminated by the shimmer stone on my desk. The books and other items around my room cast pointed shadows on the walls and ceiling. Reminding me there is much more to people then just appearances.

I drape my arm over my eyes. There is much more to Thane than I ever realized. Is he the one who sent the message, with the incorrect page number? Or was it someone else wanting to sabotage my work? Thane has been getting more and more distant from me since magic reappeared in the world.

He seems to be angrier and more urgent in his actions. He has always been patient with me, but now he is far from it. He must know about my traitorous actions, which makes me reconsider my mission. Maybe it was a test of loyalty to ensure I still follow him without question.

I know I keep making up my mind, saying I want to change, but I always come running back to Thane. It's true that every time I betray him, I end up hurting myself and others, but this time? This time I listened to him. And now? Now, I not only hurt Sophia, but the elves, and even the boy. Heat prickles my cheeks.

I slide my arm off my face and focus on the ceiling. I don't know who I am anymore. Before it was so simple, I was

Kiara, right hand to Thane, the leader of Gemini and future king of all of Ulterra. Now, now I don't know if I should call myself Kiara. What would my brother think if he saw me now? I'm sure he would ask where his little sister went – something I don't think I would be able to answer.

The thought crushes me like the weight of a roaring waterfall. I curl up, wrapping my arms around my legs. What have I done? I don't deserve to live anymore. I have allowed people to run wild, killing and stealing, I have let people die in front of me without a care, I've…I've killed, all in the name of peace and happiness. That's a laugh! How is there peace as long as people are killing? How is there happiness when people live in fear for their lives and their property? Yes, it's true we aren't ruling with fear and force, but total subservience because people have lost everything that makes humans great – creativity, dreams, imagination – isn't any better!

I sit up and stare at my dresser, a mirror reflecting the shimmer stone's light. It outlines my figure and casts a little light on my face. My eyes are dark and cold and most of my hair appears muddy. But the light casts a glow on it, enhanced by the natural golden color of my hair. The darkness is growing in me, but I can't let it win.

I shift forward and sit on the edge of the bed, still staring at the mirror. My movement lets light shine off the necklace I always wear, silver lightning bolt with a gemstone in the center. I grab it tightly. This necklace was a gift from my brother on my eighth birthday. He spent almost a year's wages on it, but he said it was worth it. I asked him why a lightning bolt and he laughed. I will never forget his words,

You're like a bolt of lightning, Kiara. You're fierce and unpredictable, but you're bright and mesmerizing. You light up the dark and remind people of the greatness in the world.

I thought they were cheesy words at the time, and Ewan did as well, but they stuck with me. And they will always stick with me. I shake my head. Sometimes I forget how much of a dork my brother could be. I look back in the mirror and see the smile on my face, and the glow of the necklace he gave me. For the first time in a long time, everything feels right. There is no storm raging inside me. I'm finally one.

I know what I must do.

I step out into the dimly lit hall. It's quiet. My goal is to find Thane and to stop this madness. Maybe we can find another way of doing things. If he fails to listen to reason, force may be the only way to stop him. It seems to be his favorite course of action as of late.

I march through the halls, head held high, not because I need to feign confidence, but because for the first time, I am confident. I pass a few hooded people. They slightly bow their heads in acknowledgement of my rank. I ignore them as I always do. I can't let anything stop me.

I round a corner and the faint scent of the sea hits me. I smell the brine of the ocean, mixed with seaweed. It's an odd smell to find in an inland area. Though, if members came back from a trip near or on the ocean, it would make sense. Their clothes must have clung to the scent. I peek my head around the corner and look into the hall that leads to Thane's study.

There are two figures, one hooded and the other is Ralph. Salt stains the bottom of the unknown man's cloak. He seems familiar with Ralph. The pair speaks in hushed tones, but they are too engrossed in their conversation to notice me. I hide behind the corner and strain to listen in.

"…no luck," unknown says.

"That's ok. Just keep up your investigation," Ralph says. His deep voice struggles with whispering.

"Other…news…" I lean a little closer to them and still my breaths. I am sure the figure is male, but his voice is so light I can only hear the occasional word.

"That is interesting," Ralph nods.

"…interception…" unknown says.

"Thank you for the report. I'll make sure Thane gets the news."

I peek around and see the figure nod. He then turns toward me and walks. I force myself out of the corner like I was just walking this way. I look as the figure passes, but he keeps his head low and his hood pulled far over his head. The smell of the sea tickles my nose as he walks by. I guess this man's mission was somewhere near the sea.

"Kiara," Ralph nods at me.

"Ralph," I nod, "I would like to speak with Thane, is he in?"

He leans against the rock wall and examines me. I keep my chin high as I stare at him.

"He's not."

I cross my arms. This isn't what I wanted to hear. "Where is he?"

"Out," he grunts.

I glare. "Where is he?" I repeat.

He returns the glare. "Kiara, he's busy."

I feel a strange sensation. I'm not quite fuming, but I'm not happy.

"Glare at me all you want. I'm still not going to help you."

"He's in another story, isn't he?" Ralph's brows rise momentarily. Bingo. I take a step toward the study.

The feeling in me grows stronger. It's reminiscent of when I work with wind and fire, but it's slower, stronger.

"Don't do this, Kiara."

The feeling grows stronger still. "He's using quartz and dragon's eggs, isn't he?"

Ralph clenches his jaw and looks away.

"You told him the dangers, didn't you?" I ask, starting to lose strength and turning to desperation.

"We did. But he doesn't care. He says we are so close, it's worth the risk." Ralph looks truly pained by this. He may be Thane's subordinate, but I'm sure they consider each other friends.

I shake my head, tears threatening my vision. I take another step toward the study. Ralph pushes himself off the wall.

"Kiar-" he grabs for me.

"No!"

Rock jets out of the wall and wraps itself around Ralph, pulling him back to where he was standing. My eyes go wide. Earth, of course. I slump a little, feeling drained, but I turn away. I march toward the study and leave Ralph struggling with his binds.

I summon wind and blow the wooden doors open. Some papers fly off Thane's table, chairs shift, and books fall open. But Thane isn't in here. I walk to his supply case on the right wall and dig through the box. Empty. He took the whole supply of quartz with him. I chuck the box at the wall with a shout.

"Mirror, show me Thane," I shout.

The image sputters into sight, despite my lack of gestures. Though I will have a nice one for Thane when I get my hands on him. So much magical energy absorbed by someone with no abilities of their own – he's going to get himself killed! I may be pissed because I was used, but I don't want him dead. He still took care of me when I had no one. I have to save the world from him, then I need to save him from himself. It's unnatural for someone to use the magic of so many dragon eggs, especially in such a short amount of time.

I huff and puff enough to calm my blind rage so I can finally observe the image in the mirror.

Thane stands on a balcony made of ebony material. His hood is down, but he still dons his shadow cloak. In front of him is a great expanse, a cliff in the distance with trees on it. The image shifts a little and shows a dark army in front of him, waiting for orders. He lifts his arms and seems to get howls from his minions. I pick up a nearby chair and hurl it at the mirror.

Splintering wood and shattering glass mix together with my scream. I turn and storm out of the study, whirlwinds picking up glass, wood, and papers, are left in my wake. I march past Ralph who has stopped moving and watches me as I near him. When I pass, he struggles again and calls after me. I can't hear him over the thump of my pulse.

I continue my march toward Gareth's study. His study is where I have most of my lessons about everything, except fighting. If he isn't in there, then he'll be in the connecting library. It's taken years, but Thane and I have amassed an impressive library. I thought it was simply because I love reading, but I know better now. It's because he needs the stories and their magic. He told me it was our job to protect the books. But now I understand he wanted to keep the magic for his followers and himself. He would destroy copies. I never truly understood anything that man did, or does.

I blow into Gareth's study. The old man jumps and throws his hands on all of the papers in front of him, trying to keep them from flying away. Once the wind dies down, he looks up at me.

"Kiara, what is the meaning of this?" he asks, authority mixed with desperation.

I give him a cold, steely gaze. "Where is the book?" I ask.

His eyes grow wide. "Kiara, what is going on?"

"Gareth, where is the book?"

He keeps his eyes on me and hands me the open book in front of him. I match his gaze and take the book from him. I turn around and scour the open pages.

Clara marches into the forest, the strength of an unknown force guiding her forward. She must save Prince Hyram before it's too late! The man certainly can handle himself, but he must be reminded that she can as well. This isn't a battle for one person to wage, not when it's against one's own kin.

Clara's fairy and gnome friends rush out to join her as she continues her stride deeper into the forest. She has a sharp mind and a strong power; nothing will stop her. She will show the brothers just how strong she really is.

Clara? Wasn't that the name of the woman in that manor? I shake my head, that isn't going to help me. A forest. There was a forest in the distance of where Thane is. Perhaps that is where Clara is entering. I wave my arm and open a portal.

"Wait! Kiara, please!" Gareth shouts, reaching out for me.

I turn to give him an icy look before I enter the vortex. I take a few more steps and he pulls me back. I whip around and glare at him.

He lets go and shrinks back. Then he straightens up again. "Kiara, this is from Thane. He told me to give it to you were you determined to follow him." I rip the note from the old man and head back for the portal. "Wait." I turn to stare at him. "Please be careful." I nod and enter the vortex.

Thane, you're a jerk.

Chapter 12

I step out into the middle of a thick forest. Brush crunches under my boots and a brush snags my cloak. This is nowhere near as thick as the forest in *A Seed of Courage*, nor is it as humid. There is a trail nearby and I wade through the brush to get onto the better terrain. I scan the area, unsure where Clara and her "friends" might be. I suspect these friends of hers are actually the idiot boy and the others. I dust myself off and charge in the direction I pray leads deeper into the forest.

I eventually come across a sign in a fork in the trail. I sigh and study it. I don't know where I'm going or how to get there. Then, I remember the note Gareth gave me before I left. I reach in my pocket and pull out the note, Thane's careful script across the front.

Kiara,

Odds are you are going to find out what I've been doing and you'll come after me. I left this note with Gareth since I know you'll go to him searching for the copy of A Fighting Chance.

You're probably upset that I ignored your warnings about the quartz and dragon eggs, but it had to be done. Despite a lot of back peddling, we have done thanks to the moronic boy and his friends, I think I have figured out the solution to end this and end it now.

Knowing you, you probably won't read this note until you're in the story and looking for how to reach me. I've drawn a map on the other side of this note. The only way I'm leaving here is when my work is done. So, please come help me. The sooner we're done, the sooner I leave here. And I promise I won't touch quartz or dragon eggs ever again.

-Thane

Oh yes, don't be mad at Ralph, he did try to stop me.

I glance at the map on the other side and commit it to memory before I crumple the note and throw it to the ground. I'm not falling for any of that crap anymore. As soon as I reach the castle, I'm dragging his sorry hide back to HQ with me.

I look back at the sign post. The map told me to continue on straight, but the sign post is telling a different story. Either the map is wrong or someone messed with the –

A shout shatters my thoughts. I check my surroundings and take off to the left most path. Someone is in trouble and I can bet Thane had something to do with it.

I sprint on the path, the lush trees turning sickly as I press forward. It's only natural someone sent Clara to this area. I shake my head. Looks like Thane will have to wait. It would do me no good to drag his butt out of here if the protagonist dies before the end of the story.

I get close to the commotion and leap into the brush, trampling around in the leaves and twigs. I stop behind the thickest, ashen tree I can find and listen.

I hear a female groan as what sounds like a body hits the ground. I peer around the tree and see the white-haired elf and the idiot boy on the ground. My eyes widen. It can't be. There is another woman there, the image of perfection, a stark contrast from when I last saw her. Clara stares up at the branches above. I scan the ground, but I see no sign of the Va'ahn or the short haired elf. I follow Clara's gaze and see the missing team members hanging in the tree's grasp.

A magical tree? Preposterous.

The tree swings some branches as if it is taunting the boy.

The boy stumbles to his feet and staggers toward the elf on the ground. He picks up the glowing sword the elf was holding moments before. Then the power drops from it, turning it back into a stick. I pull my head back behind the tree and stifle a laugh. He really is pathetic!

When I have my laughter under control, I peek back around. Wooden creaks most famous in creepy old manors sound around everyone. I quickly glance around the area to make sure I'm still safe. Sick, ashen trees, still as the grave, stand around me. No sign of life, from the trees or otherwise. A quick sigh of relief as I turn back to watch the scene unfold.

The tree makes an attempt to grab the boy, and misses. He continues dodging with inhuman speed. The earth is turned up wherever the branches land, but it doesn't faze him. He continues his movements, even as another branch launches toward him. He leaps, landing on the branch and swiftly jumps to the next nearest one. He continues his journey upward and swings the weakly powered sword through the branch holding the Va'ahn. The tree lets out a willowy scream.

The wind rushes from my lungs as I watch the creature fall to the ground. I cringe as the Va'ahn lands with a dull thud. I look back and see the idiot is still climbing toward the elf. I can't catch my breath as I watch him jump from branch to branch. He has to save her! He leaps again, ready to take out the final branch.

Then the tree pulls all its branches up, including the one holding the elf, causing the boy to fall to the earth. He lands on his back and doesn't move. My pulse quickens, the dull thud echoing in my ears. I don't know what to make of the scene. No one moves.

I hear the elf in the tree muttering something to her friends, but it's too low for me to hear. The boy is on his feet, stumbling around, waving the stick at the tree like a madman. The elf in the tree isn't moving. The elf on the ground frozen in place, like her worst nightmare is coming true. Something is breaking inside her.

Clara tries to stop the boy from waving his stick around and to move on. She manages to pull him along and the Va'ahn nudges the elf to move forward.

I run out a few steps from my hiding place. They can't! They can't just give up and leave her behind! That's not what family does. The boy turns back and I hit the ground. I try to still my breaths. He almost saw me. I slam my fist into the dirt and leaves. A sting vibrates through my wrist from the impact.

After a few minutes of lying on the uneven ground, I slowly pick my head up and check to see if the group is gone. I bring myself to my knees when I see the area is empty. I stand, dusting off dead leaves and dirt from my cloak.

If they're not going to save her, then I am. I summon my staff, the polished wood comfortable in my palm. Now, how to deal with the tree?

Chapter 13

A gust of wind softens my landing. I drop to my feet, panting. This stupid tree, why won't it just die? I have been fighting it for far too long.

The elf hasn't stirred since the others left, so it's pretty safe to say she doesn't know I'm here. But I can't help but spare her a glance every now and then. I need to make sure she is still breathing or this whole effort would be pointless.

An idea pierces my muddled thoughts, but I shiver it away. I know it would work, but there's got to be other options.

The tree swings a few more branches at me. I hop backwards, easily dodging the arms. Please, I trained with Ralph, and he put me through worse, even when I was sick. This is nothing. I could keep this up all day.

Thing is, I don't have all day. Thane is expecting me to join him. And I am eager to meet with him. He's got to stop all this madness.

The tree sends another few branches toward me, trying to hit me out of the forest. Dodging them is easy, but increasingly infuriating. This tree isn't even treating me like a threat, it's just swatting at me like an annoying gnat. I get a frosty feeling in my chest at the thought.

I'm tired of being underestimated. Sure, people revere me, being Thane's right hand and all, but they don't truly believe I deserve the position. And that boy! I'm not jealous, but Thane has been searching for him for a while. What makes him better than me?

My temper flares with the surrounding atmosphere – a searing, blinding rage. That boy is not better than me. I lift my hands in front of me, anger driving my motions. I focus on the fact that people see me as inadequate. Oh, I'll show them. Flames burst from my hand and shoot toward the tree.

The unearthly howl from the tree pulls me from my rage. I instantly drop my arms and the flames cease, including the ones burning the tree.

"Oh, my gosh," I mutter into my hand.

I didn't mean to actually burn the tree. I just wanted to stop it and get the elf back. The tree twitches in pain, dropping the elf in the process.

Instincts overcome me and I run to catch the elf. Yet another stupid decision on my part. The short-haired elf lands on top of me, still completely unconscious – the only benefit out of the whole encounter.

I pull myself out from under her and stare. The tree has stopped moving, probably resting and healing itself. The elf appears to have been singed a little from the flames. I could have hurt her, just like I hurt Ralph. I twinge, numb with fear of what could have happened.

I am never using fire again.

Chapter 14

Once I move the elf out of reach of the tree, and figure out a way for her to reunite with the others, I head off in the direction Clara and the others went.

The trees are still pretty sickly looking, but as I continue on, they seem to be getting healthier, much to my relief. I couldn't stare at the ashen trees anymore. They remind me too much of the destruction fire leaves behind.

Oh, God! I almost killed someone. I shake my head, getting rid of my tears and pulling my mind from those hazy thoughts. Just in time too, since it seems a dense fog has rolled in.

I stop in time to hear shouting. Looking around I jump for cover behind a nearby tree. Even though I'm sure no one can see me through this fog, I can't run the risk of someone accidently running into me.

"We are not leaving without Ethra. She is coming with us."

I involuntarily roll my eyes. The boy got yet another person in danger. It's so infuriating to think Thane was searching for him for so long. If he would have found him, I'm sure we would have been killed ages ago.

Haunting voices protest against something. The fog almost seems to be moving, quickly and with purpose.

"Stop that!" one of the voices shouts. There is such fear in her voice, whatever the boy has planned can't be good.

But what are these things? I can't see anything through the fog.

More protests sound. Whatever is going on, they are focused on the boy. If I could clear the fog, even just for a moment, I could see what's going on. I summon a gentle gust into the thick fog, one soft enough no one would think much about it.

The gust goes far enough to show a shadowy figure before it fades. That figure had to be the boy, but then what could he possibly be struggling against? The fog continues to swirl and move, thinning out near me, but getting thicker near where the boy is standing. It's like the fog has a mind of its own, as if...

I cover my mouth to stifle a gasp. This isn't normal fog. It's the nieblafae. I remember reading about them in Gareth's journal of creatures. I have always been captivated by the haunting face that was sketched in there. The nieblafae can be dangerous, like sirens, but they have the ability to hurt those on land and sea, anywhere fog can appear.

Something sparks from within the fog. It takes me no time to know I need to shield my eyes. I spin on my heel and face away, just in time to avoid getting blinded by the intense light. The trees around me light up, but not from a fire. This is just pure light.

Screeches sound all around the area, a signal that the nieblafae have lost whatever battle they were waging. The light, along with the screams and the fog, fades, revealing a marshy area and three figures. I'm relieved to see the Va'ahn is still here. Clara is ok as well. The boy is on the ground, rubbing his neck, like something had him in a choke hold moments before. That idiot! The nieblafae are *fog* people. They can return. He needs to move.

A muffled shout pulls me from these thoughts. No. It's just not possible. It can't be. A frightening cool comes over me. The other elf, Ethra if I heard correctly, is missing. The boy looks around frantically as another bang and shout sound from somewhere nearby.

"Ethra!" he shouts, pain filling his voice.

The group starts searching around frantically, though there really isn't anywhere for the elf to hide. The banging tells me she isn't hanging in the air or under the water, unless…

"Zev, over here!" the Va'ahn shouts.

My heart stops. The boy runs over and falls to his knees at the edge of the murky water. She's trapped. The elf is under the water. I feel my lungs fill with water, like I'm trapped right along with her. I grab the tree. No, I'm here. I'm fine.

The boy sticks his hand in the water to pull Ethra out. I continue holding my breath. He's got to get her out of there. Then, Clara runs forward and pulls the boy away from the water. Fury prickles my skin, that is until I see why she did it.

"What was that for?" the boy asks with an inhuman snarl.

She says something inaudible to me, but I can guess at what she's trying to say to him. I watch in horror as the boy's almost skeletal hand repairs itself, flesh wrapping around muscle. That's no ordinary water.

No, it's not just water, it's a portal to another world. And there is only one place, off the top of my head, that takes life from you when you enter.

The World of the Dead.

The Va'ahn says something and stares back out across the marsh, his eyes seeing far beyond this area.

"But, what about Ethra? How-How is she?" the boy asks, losing any calm he had, not like it was much to begin with.

"The nieblafae must have the ability to drag bodies in without damaging them. It could be a spell. It doesn't matter though, you were nowhere near saving her," Clara explains.

A spell? That shouldn't be too bad, especially for a High Sorceress.

"But…" the boy looks frozen.

"She's right…preserve Ethra…between worlds…no way…" I strain to hear the Va'ahn, but his voice has grown soft in despair.

Another exchange happens. The boy is starting to get hostile towards Clara. He stands and steps toward her gesturing at her, frantic to get her to do something.

"I can't! Don't you think I would have by now if I could?" Clara shouts. "I can't use magic! I can't!"

Impossible. Of course, she can. I don't know much about the story, but I know she can use magic.

The boy turns back toward the swamp. He's starting to get nervous, much like how Ethra got fidgety when she saw her sister stuck in the trees grasp.

"NO!" the boy shouts. He sticks his hand in, his face scrunched with pain and determination. He's going to save his friend, even if it costs him an arm, or more. His arm makes it deeper in before Clara pulls him back again. The boy falls back and the woman holds him.

I involuntarily twitch. The boy holds his hand up and blankly watches as it reforms, slowly. He really was going to risk everything to save his friend this time.

Once Clara is sure the boy won't make a third attempt to rescue his friend, she helps him to his feet and leads him away from the area.

I watch as the trio stumbles away. It's not until they are out of sight that I step out from behind the tree.

Now, it's my turn.

Chapter 15

I look down at the ethereal elf. She lays under the water, the image of serenity, save for the other bodies in the water. Her hair floats around her like a halo. Tears fill my eyes and I blink them away. Yes, sure this is a sad scene, but I have no reason to cry. Especially, because I am sure I can still save her.

Two things are on my side. It's water, like Gareth said, my element. The other, this is a story, and I have learned I can change a few things if it pleases me. I just need absolute focus, and maybe a prayer or two.

I whip my staff out, not in any hurry to repeat the boy's skeletal show, and dip it carefully in the water. I see the wood is still in one piece and I push it further in, testing the waters as it were. Then something jerks the staff down, causing me to stumble a half a step. I yank the staff out in response. As it leaves the water, so does a water-logged, skeletal hand.

Vegetation drops off it as it lifts higher out of the water, refusing to let go of my staff.

I give my staff another tug and break it free from the thing's grasp. I pant in relief. Well, at least I know I can reach the World of the Dead. I look back at the elf, who is still in her peaceful slumber. If that little episode didn't wake her, I'm not sure much else will.

I need to either pull her out myself, or wake her up and get her to hold onto the staff. There is no guarantee either will work. Just because my staff can reach her, doesn't mean I can. Perhaps if I'm holding onto my staff, I'll be able to reach her. Of course – I glance at Ethra's neighbors – I might need to deal with them.

I tap my foot impatiently, waiting for the solution to hit me.

"What if…?" I say out loud. "Hmmm…"

I take a deep breath and kneel in front of the water where the elf is.

"Ok, water, let's do this," I say.

I hover my hands over the water and push down. I stop right before my fingers touch the surface, but nothing is happening. Well, little ripples are forming, but it's not quite what I need. I concentrate, summoning a wind barrier on my hands and push down again.

The water finally starts pushing away from me, clearing a spot as I reach deeper. Now for the seriously challenging part, I've got to make sure I can reach Ethra in this other world. I exhale and focus, imagining I'm reaching through an invisible barrier.

The water continues to recede from where my hands are and I finally see what I've been looking for, Ethra's hands. I lean further over the edge of the water. I can't pull her out by just her hands. I gulp and reach around her waist. A slight burning sensation tingles my hands. I breathe through it and pull, focusing on getting the elf, and myself out of the water.

To my relief she is moving with me, though, to my horror, so are the other watery figures. I speed up my rescue and topple backwards with the unconscious Ethra. But my nightmare isn't over yet. Hands, arms, and heads are starting to lift out of the water.

"Oh, crap," I breathe.

Whatever I did, I broke the barrier between worlds. That barrier may have been as much for the living's protection as it was a trap for the dead.

I pull the elf away from the water's edge and prepare for battle. My staff materializes in my hands, comforting me. I can do this.

One of the ghastly skeletons starts hoisting himself onto land. I shoot a wind gust at him, knocking him back in the water. Yeah, I can do this.

Something plops behind me, and I am faced with even more skeletons raising out of the water. They want to take the elf back, and probably me as well.

I clench my jaw. That boy owes me for this.

I run toward the nearest skeleton and knock it away with my staff, it stumbles back, but not far enough. I ignore it for a beat and send a wind blast at two skeletons to my left. It knocks one off at the knees, its upper body flying back toward the water. The second skeleton falls to the ground.

Something grabs my shoulder, and I meet the watery face of the partially decayed skeleton I attacked first. Its flesh looks as if it is melting off its bone, making me want to hurl. I force the sensation down and spin, knocking him down with my staff.

This move allows me to see more figures coming out of the marsh on the opposite side. Oh, hell, what have I gotten myself into? If I would have obeyed Thane, this wouldn't be happening.

No. If Thane wasn't trying to destroy stories, this wouldn't be happening.

I look back down at the unconscious elf. Her sleep looks uneasy now, but at least she is still breathing.

I push forward sending wind blasts and swinging my staff at the figures as they keep coming. I keep having to turn an eye toward the elf to make sure she is ok, or if she is awake This would be so much easier if I only had to worry about myself, or if the other person present was conscious.

Another wind blast sends a particularly putrid smelling skeleton back into the water. Wind is the easiest for me to command, but water is *my* element. That must be the answer to this.

I huff. If this doesn't work, I'm going to have to make a tough decision – my life, or neither of us lives.

I move close to Ethra. With a deep inhale, I summon a whirlwind. Ethra remains safe, but the skeletons aren't so lucky. The raging wind tears the decayed flesh from the bones and breaks the bodies apart. The pieces soar around, occasionally being spit back into the water.

An exhale ends the torrent, throwing the remaining bits into the water. I focus with another breath, allowing me to distinguish between the waters swirling in the muck around me. I sensed it when I was pulling Ethra out, but now I'm sure of it. I can't explain it, but I feel two different waters in the swamp around me. It's almost like "my water and their water" – the waters of life and the river of death.

I run over to the water in front of me, keeping my mind on pushing the river of death back down where it belongs, and out of the path of the living. I tap the surface of the water with the bottom of my staff and the water stills. I glance back down and see the decayed army has stopped fighting and they have returned to their not-so-eternal slumber. I do the same to the other side, relieved no more skeletons climbed out while I was trying to separate our worlds.

I plop down next to the unconscious Ethra. The World of the Dead, here in this story, stranger things have happened. According to Gareth, and really all of Ulterra, the World of the Dead is real to us. But I'm sure it wasn't in this story. No, I can't be sure until I get back and pick up a copy of the book. What I don't get is that not just anyone is supposed to be able to reach into that place.

A rustle gets my attention as a thin deer steps out of the forest. It bends its head to drink from the murky water. I cringe at the thought of what is in there, but to my surprise, the creature appears unaffected by the water. Whatever was affecting the boy, causing his hand to decay, isn't hurting the deer.

I cautiously crawl to the edge of the water and stick a finger in. The cool water dances around my skin, along with the dirt and bits of foliage. I pull it back out and examine the water dripping off my normal, healthy finger. Summoning a little power to control water, I can still sense the flow of the river of the dead, but it's back where it should be.

If the water doesn't affect people normally, then why did it hurt the boy? And why was a skeleton able to grasp my staff? The only difference in our actions and the one of the deer and my finger test is that we weren't trying to reach for the dead. We were just feeling the water of the living.

Two waters, actions and thoughts…if I eliminate the fact that we are human and it only affects humans, something disproved by my finger, then…it can't be possible. No, that boy can't…but I've eliminated the impossible, so despite the idea being improbable, the boy has a gift. He has a gift like mine.

A lightness fills my mind as I try to piece grasp my dawning realization.

A moan next to me shuts my thoughts down as I stare at the elf next to me. She moves a little and stops again. A restless slumber, to my relief, but she will probably wake up soon, which means I need to get out of here.

I doubt anything will come and get her. Whatever attack the boy used, it definitely did a number on the nieblafae. As long as she moves before morning, she should be ok.

I re-summon my staff for one last go in the area. I hold it carefully as I drag it through the sodden ground.

Went ahead to the castle.

←

I draw an arrow in the direction the trio headed. This will have to do. Now all I have to do is pray there are no other problems so I can get to Thane and stop this madness.

Chapter 16

I stumble along, off the beaten trail as it were. Though I wish there were a trail. My only relief is that the trees have returned to normal and the sound of forest dwellers has returned. The fallen leaves and underbrush swish and crunch as I trudge forward, stepping carelessly. This is what a forest is supposed to look like. A bird flies from a lower branch to another tree, startled by my reckless approach. A sign of life, thank goodness. All the death was starting to get to me. This has been one hell of a crazy detour.

Of course, if I didn't take this path, the elves would have been left for dead. That idiot really needs to take better care of his friends....

"Now, now Ma 'dam, please let me go. I have told your son several stories. I am very delighted he is so thrilled to hear the story of Susan, the Va'ahn of Change, and my great, great grandmother, but please, I really need to be rejoining my group. They are probably completely lost without me."

I stop, fear taking hold of me.

That voice.

I know that voice.

I try, to the best of my ability, to approach the small clearing as quietly as possible. I find a sizeable boulder on a ledge and make a roundabout trip for it.

"Well, if my little boy is happy, then it should be ok," a female voice bellows.

I peek out from behind the rock and the scene below makes my temper flare. Three. The boy lost three of his companions. The elves may have been able to free themselves, but leaving the Va'ahn behind is unforgivable. I dig my fingers into the mossy rock, trying to find an outlet for my growing frustration.

"Another story!" a child's voice cries.

"But Madam-"

"Now, now, Tyre dear, the boy wants another story," the woman cuts the Va'ahn off.

Tyre lets out an exasperated sigh. I peek back out from behind the rock after getting my anger in check. I have accepted the situation, so now it's time for me to do something about it.

The Va'ahn begins a story about Harold, the wood gnome, something I think I remember reading when I was younger. I wish I could listen to the story, but I'm sure it's getting late.

There are three figures sitting among a mud pit, well two in the mud pit and a mud caked Va'ahn stuck to the ground at the edge. My heart goes out to him. Mud is not fun, nor does it smell pleasant. It will be worse when it completely dries, he won't be able to move an inch.

The two in the mud are also covered, from head to gloppy bottom. One figure towers as tall as these ancient trees and the smaller figure is about the size of a horse. The taller figure has rocks and cattails sticking out of its head, reminiscent of a crown.

"No, a different story," the tall figure commands, "We don't like wood gnomes. They are vile creatures in these parts. Do you know any stories of the Mud People?" The figure gestures as she talks, mud dripping off her arm as it moves.

Wait. They aren't covered in mud; they are made of mud.

I let out a frustrated sigh. I can't catch a break today.

"Mud People…" Tyre ponders, "I may have a story, but I don't remember the whole thing." The Va'ahn taps his chin with his tail in thought.

"Make it up!" the young mud boy exclaims.

Great, I know Va'ahns struggle in the creativity department.

But what do I know of Mud People? They're made of mud. They are generally nice people, well, beings.

"Once upon a time, there was a young mud boy…" the Va'ahn starts.

They are highly intelligent, but are often fixated on a certain aspect of a creature's given traits.

"He was a strong, bright, young boy, with a wonderful mother."

The boy chuckles.

The book I read said there was a reason they should be avoided, or at least dealt with in the greatest care, but why was that?

"They were so wonderful, they helped a young Va'ahn, who had strayed from his friends, find them again so that he may save the kingdom. Ney, the world!"

That's it! Once they make a request, they get agitated when…

"I. Told. You. No." the Queen enunciates.

Dammit.

The young boy starts crying at his mother's change of tone. The Va'ahn tries to jump back out of surprise, but finds the mud is greatly limiting his movements.

"But ma'am, I haven't finished the story," Tyre says.

"Then finish it," the Queen challenges.

The Va'ahn nods, "the Va'ahn was reunited with his friends who all returned to share their adventurous tales with the bright, young boy, and his lovely mother."

I smack my forehead. Va'ahns are smart, but not necessarily clever.

Everything freezes for a moment before all hell breaks loose. The Queen lets out an angry bellow, like a cornered giant, ready to fight to its last breath. The ground quakes like it fears what is coming next. The mud from the area behind the figures shoots into the sky, spitting out debris at the last moment. Most of the twigs and stones fall toward the Va'ahn who is desperately trying to move out of the way. I duck behind the boulder and cover my head, protecting myself from the other debris and splashes of mud.

"Ma Ma, what happened to him?" the boy asks after everything has settled.

"Looks like he's taking a nap, dear," the Queen responds.

I whip around to see what she means by "nap" and find Tyre on the ground, not moving. Panic paralyzes me. He-he-he can't be dead. I don't see blood, but blood doesn't have to be present for someone to die. No, no he can't be dead. I'm just panicking, that's all.

I stand next to the boulder, staring down at the scene. The sensation of magic between me and an element tickles my hands and feet, but I ignore it. I need to help Tyre. He can't be dead. He's just unconscious, that's all.

The sensation grows and I start feeling weary. Yes, I'll negotiate with the Queen and will have Tyre on the right path again in no time. There won't be anything wrong, save for a headache.

The mud Queen gingerly picks up Tyre to examine him.

"We need to tuck him in, he might get a cold if we don't, Ma Ma," the princeling suggests.

"Yes, that is right. Let's take him back to the palace, dear," the Queen says, still inspecting the unconscious creature.

She's not convinced he's just sleeping, and that makes me angry. This is her fault! If she could have held her temper back, Tyre would be fine. She should know about Va'ahns, I mean, who doesn't? The magic sensation gets heavier, like my feet are rooted in the ground.

The mud Queen turns around and begins descending into the mud, like she is descending a set of stairs. The little boy totters after her.

Oh no, she's not getting away with the Va'ahn. If she doesn't know how to treat them, then she has no right to keep one as counsel. No. I rather leave Tyre with the boy then with her.

"Ma Ma, what's going on?" the boy asks in panic.

"I-I don't know, dear," the woman says.

I ignore their comments, blind with growing frustration.

"Ma Ma!"

"What? Her! She-"

Then all conversation ceases and I drop to my knees, gasping for breath.

What just happened? Why am I so tired?

The first thing I note is that I no longer feel tied to an element. I look back at the figures in front of me, both hard, the moisture from the mud gone. The boy is waist deep while his mother is up to her chest, holding the Va'ahn a few feet off the ground.

I-I-I must have manipulated the earth without knowing it. A shiver of fear passes through me, followed by utter exhaustion. Using the power of earth always leaves me drained. I guess, on a subconscious level, I knew the obvious solution. Being made of malleable earth has its advantages, but when faced with someone with the power of earth, it has major drawbacks.

I smile to myself, sleep coming fast. I shake my head and surge to my feet. I've got to get Tyre out of here before anyone wakes up. I know the Queen and her son will be fine and moving again in no time. Just like the nieblafae, a little moisture will have them right as rain in no time.

I run down the slope and onto the now hard mud pit. By the time I reach the Va'ahn I'm panting, proving just how tired I am. There's one easy way to get Tyre down.

I smile apologetically. "I'm sorry, ma'am, but I need to do this," I say looking at the statue.

I whip my staff out and send wind, sharp as a blade, through her wrist, causing the dry bit to drop off. Her hand falls to the ground and cracks, the fingers holding Tyre breaking off in the process. I use the tip of my staff to break the rest of the mud off the Va'ahn and start weighing my options. Well, weighing him.

My staff returns and I try to lift Tyre, another poor choice on my part. I may be able to carry his weight when I am at full strength, but I'm not. On top of that, he's fairly large for me to be moving for my size.

"Sorry," I whisper to him.

I then grab his front feet in one hand and his back feet with the other and start dragging him away, through a forest caked in mud.

〜 🌢 〜

"Uggh," I groan, standing and stretching my back out.

137

This is about as far as I can drag him. I look up and down the trail, but it's hours past sundown and darkness has taken over the area.

I sigh. Well, it looks like this is as far as he goes. I'm sure the elves will find him here, or maybe a nice traveler. If Ethra follows the path I left, and the dirt covered forest, she will find him.

I groan again as I pull my cloak out from beneath the Va'ahn. When we hit the dirt covered plane, something I suspect was a result of the Mud Queen's temper, I felt bad for dragging Tyre. He is probably going to have a lot of scrapes from being dragged. I laid my cloak down and dragged him on it for quite some distance.

I hold up the thing, trying to examine it. I'm sure my cloak is dirty and threadbare where Tyre was putting pressure on it. Yet another casualty thanks to the careless boy. I'll have to have another one made when I get back. I'm sure the seamstress will be ok with making another one.

I put the cloak back on and walk down the trail. I can't stop to rest yet. It's imperative I lose no more time getting to Thane. I hold my chin up with a renewed sense of purpose.

I'm going to stop Thane from this madness and save him from himself.

If I'm not too late.

Chapter 17

Stupid battlefield. Stupid soldiers. Stupid knights.

I ended up sleeping in a stupid meadow last night, too tired to continue on. The sun was just rising when I was woken up by a whiney and the scrape of a hoof. I tried to turn over and go back to sleep, but no, the stupid unicorn wouldn't let me. It took my hood in its mouth and moved it away from my face.

Many people would think being woken up by a unicorn would be the perfect way to start a day, but not when you have only been sleeping for three hours. I am sore, bruised, and still exhausted. I tried to shoo it away, a few more hours wouldn't hurt me, but it had the gall to cock an eyebrow at me.

"Well, young maiden, this field isn't the ideal place to sleep," he said.

No crap, stupid unicorn! But neither is the forest or anywhere else in this stupid story. I'm sure the woodland creatures were going to start singing as everyone sets about their daily chores.

God, I hate love stories.

I stomp into the ebony castle, past the guards who had to be gently thrown into the wall via wind blasts to let me pass. I can't believe I'm helping the idiot succeed. I must have cleared a straight path to the castle on my way across the battle field. Good thing I didn't bother being too discrete, I'm exhausted.

I angrily stomp around a corner in the dark, pristine castle. It's supposed to be a foreboding place, but it's welcoming considering my current mood. I scan the area, challenging someone to show up and stop me. Oh, please let someone try to stop me. I could bash their head against the wall right now. Better yet, let the boy stop me. He's the one causing me all these problems. Or, maybe I should just take my anger out on Thane. This is his fault too.

I take a left turn and march a little way before I hear a voice coming from the opposite direction. Thane's voice, I'm sure of it.

I briskly turn and march down the hall toward the voice. I turn into a narrow hall that opens into a large central chamber. Of course, Thane would be in the center of the castle, it's his favorite place.

My mood shifts when I fully take in the scene. Thane is pacing behind a central cauldron, smoking with some sort of brew. I doubt it's actually his. Thane doesn't like cooking, meals or potions. What gets me is the glass prison and the terribly beaten prince inside it. This must be Clara's true love.

I flush a little. He must be handsome, under the bruises, cuts, and the swelling of his face. Well, this is uncomfortable. The rest of the room matches the dreariness of the castle. It's dark, black with grey hues, polished marble floors and minimal decorations, mainly a few tapestries and of course the cauldron and glass prison.

"There you are!" Thane says.

I continue my walk into the chamber and head for him. Every speech I've been practicing on my journey here slips from my mind when I get a good look at him. I thought the Prince looked bad, but Thane…I may be too late. The reality constricts my heart. There is a magical reek coming from him. His skin doesn't appear to be quite his. Like he is wearing a suit, and what's underneath is something inhuman. His piercing yellow eyes, normally a golden color, glowing with power and determination, appear caustic. They read more poisonous than his behavior. It's like he is rotting from the inside out.

I steel my emotions. He may be too far gone.

"I'm sorry, Thane. I had some things to take care of," I respond.

I don't bother with hiding my disappointment in him. No time for flowery discussion. The sooner we are out of here, the better.

"No worries," he says, pulling something out of his cloak. "Get me some of his blood, the more the better."

I go for the knife momentarily, and contemplate running it through him. Maybe his thigh or something. I don't want him dead, just incapacitated so I can drag his sorry hide back to HQ. I'm sure Gareth will have a stern word for him. He knows better than to use so much magic that isn't his. I grab the knife and head for the glass prison.

I can't hurt Thane. He has always been there for me, especially when my big brother couldn't be. Tears threaten to betray my façade. I need to focus on my task.

The glass prison doesn't have any doors, but I know that isn't a problem. Glass prisons are some of Thane's favorite containment means. He has used them at HQ for unruly members who break some of our group's laws. He even locked up a young boy when I was little because the boy was picking on me. I could handle him myself, but Thane insisted on delivering the punishment. The person can't get out, despite the cage being made of glass. Every attempt to break the glass from the inside only serves to strengthen the walls.

From the outside, attacks are repelled. However, it can be broken. It takes some fierce determination, but it can be done. Meanwhile, Thane, and a few others of his choosing are free to enter and leave the prison. Some guards like to rough up prisoners for interrogation, some people enter to help heal the prisoners, then there are the people who bring food to them, or in my case, to draw blood.

The wall ripples like the swampy water of the Land of the Dead, and I walk through. I kneel down next to the Prince, holding the knife at the ready. I may not want to hurt him, but I doubt he feels the same about me.

"Hyram!" a shout rings in the chamber. Clara vaults over a balcony railing.

I jerk back in surprise, the outburst even causing the Prince to stir a little. He shifts his gaze to the new visitors. I watch as the boy vaults over an upper floor balcony and land behind Clara. I check Thane's reaction and see he isn't the least surprised at this.

"Nice of you to join us," Thane says.

The boy starts back with annoying retorts, Thane enjoying every second of it. I would roll my eyes if it wasn't for the enraged woman on the other side of the glass prison. A rumbling shakes the ground beneath me. Thane must have summoned something to help us.

Whatever Thane summoned isn't fast enough though. Clara has pulled out a book and is hurling spells at the prison walls. The walls pulse with each hit, and respond by reflecting them back at the assailant.

"Clara!" the boy says.

He is certainly panicked, and rightfully so. Thane just summoned an army of mercuriders. They act like spiders, but can't be defeated by cutting them. I watch as the boy slices one of the spiders and it falls to the ground, now two separate creatures. Periodically my view of the scene is obscured by Clara's continual onslaught. It'll be over soon enough though. She really should be focusing on herself. The mercuriders are up to her waist and she doesn't seem to care. She is so blind with rage that she'd rather see Hyram safe than save herself.

"Young lass," a weak voice says from beside me.

I look down at the Prince and see him staring at me.

"By your eyes, I can tell that you do not want this, but for whatever reason, you won't stop this."

I shake my head, not moving my gaze from him.

He closes his eyes. "I know not your reasons, but they must be as strong as steel for you to not calm this storm."

He fishes in his pocket, grunting in pain.

"You really shouldn't be moving," I say, despite myself.

He finds what he is looking for and pulls it out. Between his index finger and thumb stands a petite ring with a diamond rose on the top. It shines with something beyond magic and metal.

The Prince places the ring in my hand, pushing it firmly into my palm, and closes my fingers over it. My gaze still doesn't leave his face.

"Please, make sure Clara gets this, once I'm…when I'm…dead," the Prince says. "Tell her I loved her to my last breath."

I continue staring at him in confusion. He smiles a tired smile.

"I pray you find a love as great as mine," he says looking at Clara, who is now focused on freeing herself from the mercuriders. "There is something great in you, just like Clara, and I pray you find the one to share that light with."

With his last word, the Prince closes his eyes. Tears flow out uncontrollably. I look back at Clara and see she is completely covered. I glance at the boy and see he is nothing but a mound of mercriders. Thane is standing and observing the scene with an appraising smile.

Is this it? Is this the end of everything? The end of true love, the end of magic, the end of my journey? The glass walls around me vibrate with an unknown frequency. Tears keep pouring down my face, but I don't know why. I'm too numb for such an emotion. This is impossible. We worked for this for so long, but this can't be what we wanted.

The vibrations of the glass grow more intense, along with my emotions. My whole body is buzzing with energy, save for my clouded brain. The same thoughts repeat over and over. It's over. We are done. We won, and lost everything in the process.

"Aaaaaaaahhhh!"

Chapter 18

The calm that had come over the chamber becomes interrupted again as more bodies fill the room. Why there is fighting, I'm still not sure. Everyone who openly opposes Thane are incapacitated if not dead. All I can tell now is that I've lost control of my body. My mind is keenly aware that I'm still summoning some magic. My muscles remember this, but I don't. I've never felt this tremor, this strength. It's not foreign though, it is my energy.

Shouting rises over the clang of metal on metal. I so desperately want to see what's going on, but I can't move. Cheers sound as whatever spell I'm doing releases. I feel the release of energy come out of every pore on my body. I brace myself with my hands to stop myself from completely collapsing.

Panting mixes with the sound of shattering glass. I don't move as I feel shards rain down on me, each piece clinking as it hits the ground. What have I done?

Nearby shuffling pulls me from my frozen state. Somehow the Prince has recovered a bit, the swelling and bruises nearly gone, and he is running toward the mound of mercuriders that claimed Clara. I roll back on my heels and observe the chaos around me.

Strange armored shadows have invaded the room and are joining the battle against the Prince, the boy, the elves, and the Va'ahn. I should be relieved to see that they made it here, and a part of me is, but I still can't process everything. It's like there is some haze or filter in my head preventing me from understanding this moment.

The Prince is making surprising progress, digging through the mercuriders like they are nothing. A glimpse of a hand tells me Clara is still fighting on the inside. A burst of a strange power emanates from them. It's strong and calming. This may be why he is having an easy time plowing through the mercuriders.

The boy and his friends are engaging in battle with Thane's mindless servants. Kicks, punches, slices, and shouts come from each of the fighters as they easily overcome their opponents. What they don't notice is Thane is doing something. I've never seen a spell like this, but it's almost like he is giving the creatures his life force in order to make them stronger. He shouts in a tongue I don't know, completing his spell.

There is no way they are going to win against Thane as long as he is breathing.

I go back to watching the Prince and his efforts to save Clara. He has successfully uncovered her hand and is pulling her out of the mound. The mercuriders sizzle away in wisps of smoke, allowing Clara to gain more ground. The pair continue to work together and Clara is soon free again. There is an inexplicable look in her eyes. So many emotions are going through her, but one emotion stands proudly in front.

The two embrace and kiss, filling the chamber with the warm and calming power I felt earlier. The light is blinding, reminiscent of the light the boy used against the nieblafae. For the first time in ages, I finally feel at peace with myself and everything around me, like everything will be ok and that everything I've been doing won't be for naught.

The light soon recedes, revealing a significantly empty chamber, and a loving couple locked in an embrace. The cold, harsh reality of what I must do washes over me.

"No!" Thane shouts.

Thane is losing it. This last attack was the end of his strength. I'm too late. He raises his hands. I surge to my feet, my mind processing something I can't quite understand.

Shouts ring out throughout the room, but I don't hear them. My body has taken control again, leaving my mind and comprehension behind.

Dark wind-like blasts come soaring towards me and I whip out my staff. A flicker of a distant memory dances in my mind. I stand between the boy and the blasts and create a wind shield, deflecting the spell.

My mind then catches up.

I am chasing after a group of older boys, not yet in their teens. They are hunting down and terribly beaten boy about my age. The group enters an alleyway, and I follow. The bullies are sauntering toward their prey, tormenting him, drawing out their victory. But today is not their day. I run past them and turn to face them. My arms are out to the side as I shield the semi-conscious boy. Words are exchanged and the bullies are smirking, but their smirks quickly fade when they sense something coming from me. A magic awakening in me. They quickly back away and make a run for it. Unfortunately, the boy has passed out. I leave the alley as well and tell the first adult I see about the injured child.

"Kiara? What are you doing?" Thane asks, interrupting my memory. He is pissed.

"Stopping you," I respond with equal anger. "I've had enough of this."

"I've warned you before, you will never see your bro-"

"I don't care about that now! Why would I want to find him if we have nothing to return to?" The mention of my brother has torn down whatever hold I had on my emotions. I can't do this anymore. A whirlwind has been released inside of me and if I don't do something soon, it will rip me apart from the inside.

I pull my staff back out and blindly send wind blades at him. Growing up with the man, I should know he would deflect them. I watch as my spell hits a column to the side, rocks and debris raining down. Thane's glare bores into me, searing my flesh. Such an intense and hot anger is emanating from him.

While our eyes are locked, the boy runs out from behind me, sword in hand, and charges Thane. His anger runs hot as well, something I should have figured. He attempts to run the blade through Thane, but is waved off like a gnat. Pure strength isn't going to best Thane, not when he's like this.

Thane finally breaks his gaze with me and shifts it toward Clara and the Prince.

"They are trying to *stop* us. They are trying to take away our *happiness*, they don't *care* about your needs, your past, nothing."

I stare at him, blank faced, despite being torn inside.

"Return to my side and I will forgive your transgressions."

My transgressions. The jerk thinks I'm doing this just because I like to cause him trouble? I may be going against him, but can't he see what he is doing is hurting him as well?

"Never," I spit.

Thane doesn't seem surprised by my response, disappointed, but not surprised.

He looks away from me and grins. I know that face. He's got something up his sleeve.

"It's been fun."

No, he can't.

"I think I'll go find the real thing," Thane says as he steps into a portal.

Dammit. He did it. He left. And I know where he is going.

"He can't mean!" the boy says. "We have to go!"

I'm a step ahead of him. I open a portal near where Thane disappeared. The boy runs in without a second thought. They all run in without a second thought. I turn and give the Prince and Clara one last look. He smiles and gives me a nod and I turn and follow behind the group.

This is it, Thane. One of us won't be leaving that manor alive.

Chapter 19

I step out of the vortex and back into the sitting room I was in not too long ago. The room is still in shambles and is actually worse than when I left. Those silent assassins of Thane's really did a number on it.

The portal closes behind me and I start running toward the garden, right behind the others. I know Thane is far gone, but I need to try one more time to get him to listen to reason. We can fix all of this.

Something grabs my arm and stops me. "You're not coming."

I don't know if I want to fry the boy or knock him unconscious. I choose the best option, for him. "Like hell I'm not!"

I tear my arm out of his grip and run outside to join the others.

That boy is infuriatingly stupid. I can't stand him or his existence. I'll take care of Thane first and then maybe I'll pound some sense into the idiot.

I stop next to the other three as they stare down Thane.

My stomach flips. This is bad. This is really, really bad. Thane is no longer himself. His sharp, ever calculating eyes are distant. They dart back and forth, crazed, looking for something. He has Clara though, so I don't know what he could be searching for. His normal irritatingly annoying smile is crazed as well, and downright creepy. To top it all off, a green haze surrounds him. All symptoms of magic toxicosis.

I blink back tears.

I can't lose him. Not like this.

"Thane! Stop! Release Clara!" the boy says, stopping next to me.

Thane hears him. His eyes focus on the boy and his lips tremble like he is ready to laugh. Then, he laughs. His cackle is deranged, and terrifying. I've never heard such a sound come from him. He stops and mutters something to himself about "this story" and laughs again. He has lost it.

"They thought Prince Thane was crazy! I will show them his rule! No more differences! Subservient people, people with no will of their own! No more being left out in the cold because I am 'not good enough'! I will never abandon my people! That is why *I* will be King!"

Oh Thane…

He doubles over in laughter, releasing traces of a terrible power. He then howls in pain. My heart and resolution crumbles. Thane has always been a steady rock for me, but to see him like this…

Trying to fight back tears causes me to miss Thane's next transformation. I don't know how, but his body grows. So tall that Clara is nothing to him as he plops her on his shoulder.

"No one can stop me!" he roars.

Thane…

"He's gone mad," I finally say.

Maybe if they know he's not normally like this, they will let me handle this.

"He's absorbed too much energy. We warned him no one can handle so much magic in such a short amount of time."

I look at the boy and his deep grey eyes return my gaze. If I was naïve, I would think concern reflects in his eyes as he scans my face. He's looking for a sign that I am lying. He closes his eyes and faces forward.

"Letha! Ethra! You know what we have to do!" he barks.

"Right!" the elves say before they take off.

No. No, we can't attack him. There has to be another way. I know there is a remedy for this magic toxicosis. My breaths come in short, painful gasps as I watch the twins try to fight Thane.

No, we can't do this to him. He's not a bad person. He just made a bad choice. He did this for me, for us, for the people who came to us looking for safety from their terrible lives. No, he doesn't deserve this.

Anger starts growing in me. Why aren't they stopping their attacks?

"What do we do?" the boy turns and asks me.

I shoot him a glare. "How should I know?" I snap.

He looks surprised for a second before he says, "Well, you're his friend."

"You think he's my friend? I knew you were stupid, but seriously?" Thane is so much more than just a friend. He's been like a brother to me. He's cared for me and raised me. Disregarding everything he's done and belittling it to "friend" is insulting.

"I'm stupid? You're the one who helped a crazy man steal dragon eggs!"

"That wasn't me!" Does he seriously think I would let Thane near dragon eggs? I know how dangerous they can be and how ambitious he is. It's a deadly combination!

"I don't have time for your thick head," I say.

I stomp away from him and towards Thane. Maybe if I can show him that I don't exactly stand in unity with this idiot boy, he will return to normal.

Thane slams his palm into the ground, almost squashing one of the elves.

Well, I guess a little pain won't hurt him.

I whip out my staff and send several wind blasts toward him, just enough to get his attention.

What I didn't know is Thane has placed a protective barrier around himself. The wind bounces off of him and straight back into me.

A sharp pain in my chest takes my breath away and I fly backwards. I hit something and go tumbling with it several times before we come to a stop, with me on top. Realizing I hit the boy, I quickly get off of him and brush myself off.

I stumble back towards Thane for another go.

"Kiara! What are you doing? Get rid of this sorry lot so we can continue with our plan!" Thane says with a thunderous voice.

A realization is dawning on me, and I hate it. I tremble in fear of what must be done.

"NO!" I shout, surprising myself. "I will NEVER help you! NEVER again!"

This is not what Thane wanted to hear.

"Kiara, have they brainwashed you?"

"*You* are the one who brainwashed me! You promised happiness for everyone! A place where we can co-exist in peace! And yet you had me kill a woman's best friend! You're trying to separate Clara and Hyram. You want to destroy love. How is this *ok*?"

Something is flaring in me.

"You hurt Heinz! He did nothing wrong! He *helps* people! Why'd you have to…" I choke on a sob. I can't do this anymore.

"You foolish child, kings have to hurt people. It's the way of life. Heinz and Clara are just some of those people. As for the old man, well, he isn't fighting us anymore."

"You're terrible…"

This strikes a nerve in Thane. "Enough of this! If this is how you view my actions, then my kingdom has no place for you!"

I cry harder. I can't stop it. He's like family. No, he is the only family I have left, and I'm losing him. I fall to my knees, a weak helpless child who has just lost everything.

Why did it have to come to this? Why can't he listen to me? He always listened to every idea I ever had, no matter how strange or far-fetched. So, why can't I get through to him?

A mass flies past me, blowing my hair and cloak with it, startling me enough to stop my crying. A few yards behind me, the boy is struggling to get up after a pretty painful landing. He stands for a second before collapsing again.

I get up and run to him, meeting up with Ethra. She starts some sort of healing spell, while I do the same, calling upon water to help me. I'm not this will work, but I read about water healing spells in one of old man Gareth's many books.

It's going to work though. I'm not some helpless child. This mess is partly my fault, and I am going to do everything I can to stop Thane, here and now.

In my peripheral, another body is sent flying.

"LETHA!!!" Ethra screams. She gets up and runs away from us.

I watch her go toward her recently injured sister. Thane also watches the scene. I won't let him hurt them. I get up and run towards Thane again. I need to get his focus on me.

It works.

Thane heads for me and my eyes widen. Each step he takes is thunderous, rumbling the ground and shaking me to my core. What was I thinking? I try to devise a plan to fight him, but my mind isn't working fast enough. Thane swings his gargantuan arm at me, knocking the wind out of me and sends me flying.

I hit something again and we both fall. I look down at the boy, who despite his injuries and reservations about me just saved me. I flush at the thought of the gesture and get up. I offer him a hand and pull him to his feet. The boy dusts himself off as the twins rejoin us, Letha limping something fierce. I'm sure she wouldn't have been able to make it to us on her own.

I meet the twins and offer my shoulder to Letha to lean on. I need to see if I can heal her.

"What are we going to do now?" Ethra asks, looking at the boy.

I focus on trying to heal Letha, suppressing the urge to roll my eyes. Why does she think he would know?

Things are happening fast, and we are clearly at a disadvantage. If someone doesn't think of something soon, it could be the end of our story.

Out of the corner of my eye, I see a peach blur dashing towards us. Tyre! It finally hits me the Va'ahn has been missing in action since we stepped out of the vortex. I'm relieved to see he's safe and in relatively better shape than the rest of us.

"Zev! Everyone! I think I figured out how to weaken Thane." Tyre turns his head to point further out in the yard. "I found four pedestals over there."

Past Thane stand four terribly neglected pillars. Vines and weeds have claimed the pedestals as home in this fairly barren yard. A strange power pulses from them, almost like the pedestals are trying to breathe through the choking vines. We have to do something about them.

"How will those pedestals help us?" Letha asks.

"Well, I'm not sure how to activate them, but I remember mention of them ages ago. Back when everything was right with the world," Tyre says.

I chuckle inwardly at the thought. I can't remember when everything was right with the world.

"The pedestals were said to host four items that symbolize the strongest known magic in the world." Tyre continues.

Our world's strongest magic. Thane mentioned something like that a while ago, but what was it?

"Say we have the items; how do we know which pedestal they go on?" I ask. Old man Gareth's lessons coming back to me. "I assume there is a special sequence we have to put them in."

Everyone stares at me, blank faces, their minds far away. I turn away, uncomfortable from the attention.

"There were inscriptions on each of the pedestals," Tyre says.

"What'd they say?" the boy asks.

I half listen to the Va'ahn as he recites the pedestals' engravings. Something is still eating at me. I know Thane has discussed, at length, the strongest magic of this world. So, why can't I remember anything about it?

I tuck a strand of hair behind my ear, trying to clear all distractions from my thoughts. Let's see, there are certain stories that are the strongest in the world. Taking those out will easily crush all other stories and people's will. If the pedestals are asking for the books, like the one Thane stole from here, then we are out of luck. There is no way someone can keep Thane at bay while I fetch the story from HQ. Then there would be the issue of tracking down the other stories.

No, it would have to be something to symbolize the story. But what-!

The ground shakes, pulling me from my thoughts. I look up in time to see Thane barreling towards us. No, he can't. He's going to crush us once and for all. It would just one smack of his giant hand to flatten all of us.

Thane joins his hands together to deliver a final hit.

The wind sings sweetly, the song of our end. I close my eyes. God, save us.

The sound of lightning striking rings out and the weight of dread, and Thane, disappears. I watch as Thane flies backwards. He slides to a stop, carving a path in his stead.

Did my prayer really work? I stifle a chuckle, it's impossible. I glance at the group and the answer strikes me. The boy pulled me out of the way, trying to shield me from the impact. We all were trying to save each other. Selflessness…

"What the…?" the boy asks.

I rip my arm from the boy's grasp. "We only have a little bit of time before Thane regains consciousness."

The boy looks offended for a split-second before acknowledging the truth of my statement. "Well, the stories we visited had to deal with some sort of magic," he says.

Oh boy, he really is helpless.

"Magic that is essential to our world," Letha says.

Thank goodness for Letha. I drown the group out again. Now let's see, the pedestals aren't going to work for just any old item. These items have to be extremely unique, if not a symbol of the story, then from the –

"Of course! How simple," I say. I pull out the ring the Prince gave me. "*This* is what the fourth pedestal is talking about."

"Where did you get that?" the boy asks, suspicion clouding his steel grey eyes.

"Hyram gave it to me before I left. He said he wanted me to give it to Clara once he was…dead."

His love for Clara would be the last thought, feeling, and thing he said before he died, even after he lost the ability to fight.

I watch as the twins, in turn, share items they received from two other stories they visited. One more, we need one more item and this battle is as good as won.

"Sorry guys," the boy says.

I'm about to smack him when I see something shine under his jacket sleeve.

"This!" he fumbles with the cuff. "From Asar!"

Relief floods me. We have the four items from the oldest known stories. These have to be the items the pedestals ask for. It makes sense. We only targeted these stories after magic was released from *Dream and Disappointment.*

"I have an idea," the boy says, passing the bracelet to Tyre. He shakes himself loose. "I'll distract Thane while the four of you activate the pedestals."

He what? Before I can articulate just how absurd that plan is, Thane lets out an inhuman roar.

"No time! You guys go!" the boy says pushing me forward.

We take off running, Tyre leading the way. We decide to run the perimeter of the area, as to not draw attention to ourselves. We can't ruin the boy's plan. My anger flares. He's going to get himself killed. I think I would have been better at distracting Thane. I don't think the boy has a lick of magic in him.

No, that's wrong. When we were in the circle, when we protected ourselves from Thane's attack, I felt it.

I don't think I have felt anything like it since I shielded a boy in the alley from those bullies. No, that's wrong too. I felt it recently, when- Ouch! A sharp pain reverberates through my foot.

"You ok," Ethra asks, putting a hand on my shoulder.

I shake my head. "Yeah, thanks."

She smiles and picks up the pace. I follow her lead, embarrassed that I missed that uneven rock. I didn't fall, but the stumble did slow me down.

We round the last bush and continue straight for the pedestals. I turn my head to check how the boy is faring.

The boy got himself cornered between a stone wall and the back of the manor. Thane is grunting as he stalks toward his prey. He swings his giant arm-

Chapter 20

I scream as the boy is hit. He flies to the opposite side of the area, rolling and sliding to a stop. I can't move. I can't breathe. All I can do is watch in horror as the boy lays there, unmoving.

Letha comes back and tugs on my shoulder to keep moving, but I'm frozen. Not only can't I move, but I'm really cold, despite my cloak, despite the running.

"Come on, Kiara," she says.

I don't process anything, but the fact the boy isn't moving and Thane is coming for him. My body takes a step forward, but Letha pulls me again. I look at her and she smirks, nodding her head toward the manor.

The boy is standing, barely.

"Come on," she says again as she takes off towards the pedestals.

I give the scene one last look and follow behind her. We've got to hurry, for the boy's sake.

I reach the fourth pedestal right after Letha. We nod to each other and place our offerings, ensuring we place them at the same time. I pray that this works.

The items begin floating as they synchronize with the magic within the pedestals and the area.

We did it! These are the right items.

The pedestals pulse, knocking off the foliage and restoring themselves to brand new. The items then glow, a bright and pure golden light. The light from each item shoots up and unites in the air. A smile grows on my face as I watch the light pass through the air and towards Thane.

He howls, stepping away from the boy. The light, while welcoming to me, is killing him. My heart sinks. I wish there was another way. Thane begins to shrink back to normal size, howling as his body structure is reassembled.

The boy runs over to where Clara was tossed and I can't breathe. He drops to the ground next to her, grief pulling his shoulders down. I take off running towards the pair. We've got to heal Clara. I can't believe it's taken me this long. This is the Clara from *A Fighting Chance*.

Half way to them I can see the boy is laughing, despite him covering his face with his palm. I pick up the pace. His laugh is reminiscent of Thane's before he transformed. My thoughts race, trying to grasp something long forgotten, but I leave them be. I need to focus on stopping the boy's madness and Clara's death.

I finally reach the pair when the boy darts away, towards the semi-conscious Thane. A strange, dark power is coming from the boy, mixing with his rage and tainting the air. The boy sends punch after punch at Thane. He sends Thane flying and chases after him, like an animal playing with its food.

He's lost it. I look at the others, but they are focused solely on Clara. It's no use though. One look at her should tell them she's gone. I guess the same can be said for the boy. He's as mad as Thane.

The boy continues his barrage, Thane not even putting up a fight. It's over. We won the fight, but we lost Clara. I lost Thane. I want to scream at the boy to stop, I want this to be over. I glance at the boy and he's just sitting there now. He knows it's over too.

I start walking towards the two when giant, dark, ethereal hands come out from Thane and grab the boy around the torso. He's lifted into the air, struggling to break free. The hands then throw the boy away from the manor. I freeze again. Thane's not dead, far from it actually. Despite his grotesque looks from the beating he was receiving; Thane has never looked better. This is not the Thane I know. This power, this resilience, it's something completely different.

Thane saunters over to where the boy is laying. This will be over soon.

I blink back unknown tears.

Then, the boy stands again and charges towards Thane, shouting. He swings and a bright light consumes the area. It's not just coming from him, but everyone here. The artifact's magic is mixing with our own and it's helping the boy win. It's similar to the light that came from Clara and Hyram. But, somehow more at the same time.

The light recedes to a small shape. It struggles to maintain a form as darkness starts fighting back. I feel the struggle in my chest, like it's my own personal battle. The darkness gains ground, and the boy jumps on it, trying to suppress it. I watch as the form tries to buck the boy off.

"Zev!" I shout and take off running.

I throw myself to my knees and put my hands on his. The boy looks at me, his eyes full of exhaustion. We work together, helping the light win. A final shove and the darkness disappears, leaving a rectangular object in its wake. A deep, dark colored book.

We back away, unsure of what exactly happened. But no relief comes to us as the book shakes in place. A light springs from it and heads straight for Clara, a healing light.

We run towards her as the light finishes restoring her to pristine condition. No matter the situation, this woman is always magnificent. She examines everyone with a sure smile. Ever radiant. Ever loved.

I hang back as the others cheer her reawakening.

I can't believe it, it's over. Numbness washes over me. The wins and losses beginning to add up in my mind, leaving me with a total of nothing.

"I see you are all finally together," Clara says.

I look at her to see her gazing at me.

"What do you mean? We were together when we last saw you," the boy says.

"I will explain everything, but first…"

Clara waves her hand, combining her magic with that of the area. The pedestals hum with magic and respond to her command. Soon the whole area starts repairing itself. The broken stone walls that litter the area rebuild themselves. Glass and metal dance in the air, each going in time to an unknown symphony. It doesn't take long before the whole area is encased in metal frames. Before the glass is placed, plants, trees, shrubs, and the most stunning of flowers fly in from across the land. Some poke out of the ground, awakening after a long slumber. Once the glass is in place, a fountain, and a table with chairs appear.

Thane's book lands on a fifth pedestal and a gate shoots up around it, emanating a strong protective spell.

"That's better," Clara says.

"Clara," the boy interrupts the revelry. "What happened to Sophia? We…"

I tune him out and wander a bit closer to the nearest tree. A tree in a greenhouse? This is a bit extravagant. I reach for a leaf, but stop when I realize what this tree is. It's a tree from my hometown, from before I met Thane. It only grows in the higher altitudes. What is it doing here?

Nostalgia hits me hard as I look at the plants near it. All of these flowers and shrubs are from my hometown. My mother would tend to a small garden in the front of our house.

I can't believe it. There. Poking from the ground. Edelweiss.

Just what is this place?

"You all must be hungry. A garden party would be wonderful, given our new addition to the manor," Clara says, breaking through my thoughts.

I follow behind everyone and I am the last one sitting. I really should leave now and check on Ralph and Gareth. Someone is going to have to do something about Gemini now that Thane is detained. But I am hungry. Maybe a meal, and a little explanation, wouldn't hurt. Besides, this is my only chance to talk to the Va'ahn, now that he's conscious.

"Please everyone eat," Clara says. She begins eating with a trace of inhuman elegance.

I slouch a little in my chair. Maybe I should go. I don't belong in Lummava. I look at everyone again and catch Zev's gaze. I furrow my brows.

"Kiara, please, eat," Clara says.

I keep my eyes on the boy and he picks up his fork and starts eating, with a great struggle. I follow suit. I rather not be called out again. Being welcomed so suddenly is really uncomfortable. Unnatural even. Though, nothing here seems natural. We eat in silence, much to my relief.

After we are done here and I get some answers, and maybe a conversation with Tyre, I will slip away, back to HQ. Someone's got to relay the information about Thane's failure and the new direction we should head. Yes, that will be the pain. I put my fork down, hunger sated.

"Well, now that everyone is fed, I guess I should explain…but where to begin?" Clara thinks about her options.

"What did you mean by 'we are finally all together'?" the boy asks.

That is the other thing that has been nagging me.

"Well, there was always meant to be five of you," Clara says.

"Meaning?" the boy asks, stiffening in his seat.

"Well, you see, two of you were supposed to start this journey; however, Kiara was missing. I wondered if something happened and you weren't around anymore."

What is she saying? My heart stops. I don't belong here. If I belong anywhere, it's in Klenover, with my parents and my brother. No, I think this woman has it wrong.

"You knew you could wield magic, and well, so did Thane."

I shoot a glance at the book. *Of Darker Days* glints as if acknowledging our conversation.

"Everyone else here can wield a special power, some more obvious than others." Clara winks at the boy.

I bite the inside of my mouth and look back at the pedestals. Is she right? Do I really belong here? I slide even further down in my seat. I don't know what to think anymore.

The boy asks a question and Clara starts a long-winded explanation. I half listen to her answer. She says something about us having a gift to protect stories, that they are living things. That second part should be obvious to anyone who's read before. What catches my attention is that we are supposed to continue using our abilities to protect stories, magic, and the world. That's a bit much for me. But maybe this is what I need to do to realize Thane's dream. No. My dream.

"What do you mean 'you all'?" the boy asks.

I sit up. I didn't catch that part of her answer.

"Well, you can't expect me to live here with you. I have my own story to return to," Clara says.

This hits me hard. I know she belongs in the story, but I really can't stand the thought of her leaving. She is the reason I was able to eat with everyone without a fight. Clara gets up and heads back inside the manor.

"Clara?" Ethra asks.

The woman ignores her and picks up a book from a small table. She hands it to me, smiling encouragingly.

"Clara?" Letha asks.

I stare in the woman's ice blue eyes as a silent conversation passes between us.

I am so sorry Clara.

It's ok, Kiara. It's not your fault. You have been misguided for far too long. But no longer. Your place is here, with them.

I swallow. *No, Clara, I don't think it's right. I've done so much wrong by these people, by everyone.*

But you worked to fix it, did you not? Letha, Ethra, Tyre, and especially Zev would not be here without your help. She nods.

How?

It doesn't matter. What matters is that you want to change and make a difference. Now, please, read.

I open the book and feel as if the pages are turning themselves, getting me to the point I was intended to read, and start reading.

Good bye, Clara.

Chapter 21

I'm sitting in the main room of the manor. I think maybe it's a sun room, or was before the greenhouse addition. It took a little while, but we've cleaned the place up, back to the way it was before Thane interfered.

I flip another page of a journal when a loud bang rings out from somewhere in the house. I jump in my seat, but relax when I hear the twins' laughter. I smile and go back to reading.

A strange creature in my dream told me that I needed to come to your world and prevent a tragedy that would span the universe. I'm not entirely sure what that meant, but the urgency in its voice told me it was wise to listen.

A strange creature? I had encountered one when I was knocked unconscious. It seemed like it wanted to speak to me, but it never got the chance. Does this creature have an urgent message for me as well?

"Zev! Come on!" Letha shouts. She walks into the main room and smiles. A muffled response answers.

"Well, it's good to see you're not a slacker," she says to me.

I put the journal on the small table and meet her at the door.

"I could say the same about you," I say.

"Oh, you don't need to worry about me."

"Then I suspect the loud bang was nothing to worry about." I smirk.

She chuckles. "It was just a present for Tyre. He fell asleep in the hallway. Besides, I'm sure it woke up sleeping beauty."

We both laugh. It's taken some time, but I think Letha and I are getting along very well. We're a lot alike, in probably more ways than I even realize. I'm still getting used to her sister. Her constant joyous attitude can be annoying before breakfast. I'm not sure what to make of her carefree attitude, but it seems she isn't hiding anything behind it.

"Hi sleepy-head!" Ethra sings out from the hallway.

She is waiting with Tyre, for Zev to get down the stairs. Letha and I join her, seeing that Zev has finally decided to join us. He smirks at me and I return it with a clenched jaw. He's been acting like he won for a week since I finally caved and agreed to train him in magic. Clara is right, he has some power, but I haven't the faintest idea on what it could be. He can expect our training to be as treacherous as mine with Ralph. Maybe more.

I wonder what Ralph and Gareth are up to. The night Clara left, encouraging me to stay here with the others, I sent a letter to HQ for them, explaining what happened. I haven't heard a word since. I get the feeling they are still lurking in the shadows. Thane always had contingency plans for his contingency plans, plans that even I wasn't privy to, so they must be working on something.

We exit the manor, admiring the chilly fall day. Winter will soon be here and we're the least bit ready. We've got to find the second journal Clara wrote about. She said something bigger is coming and we best be prepared. After searching the manor, we decided it might be best to use a different tactic. This manor is far more than it appears. Every door seems to lead to more halls, doors, and questions. In the process though, I have found countless libraries, holding more books than the libraries in Klenover. I can't wait to be done with this missing journal search so I can get to reading.

But today, I'll have to settle going into town and meeting the people at the Fortune Hunter's Bureau, the Zev's guild. Maybe I'll slip away and check on Heinz instead. He wasn't hurt as badly as Thane thought. His shop was destroyed though. I've been helping him rebuild and gather new stock. A blessing in disguise really as I think I can get him to move his shop somewhere else. With the tea blends he makes, I'm sure he can afford a new, more prominent store front. I'll have to discuss this with him.

All in due time, I guess.

Acknowledgements

Wow!

We made it to the end of another entry in The Lost Library Series. Poor Kiara, she has certainly gone through quite a bit in the short time we've known her.

A big shout out to my family – I appreciate all the support and love. It means the world to me.

Another shout out to my friends! You all are so, so amazing. I appreciate the encouragement and support and time.

A third shout out goes out to the Bookstagram community! To all the other indie authors I've connected with. We've got this!

And a big thank you to you, dear reader. I wouldn't be here without you reading and supporting all the characters!

Of course, it would be remiss of me to not thank my dear characters. They go through so much. And an additional thanks for keeping me up at nights again telling me about all your antics.

I really appreciate everyone – for reading, for supporting, for sharing, and for even thinking about the series.

Stick around and see where we go from here!

About the Author

R.E.Journeys is a lover of fantasy and a friend of imagination. Journeys spends their time writing, working, and dreaming. When not doing any of that, Journeys can be found playing with the family dogs – and taking way too many pictures of them.

www.ingramcontent.com/pod-product-compliance
Lightning Source LLC
Chambersburg PA
CBHW050139110726
47898CB00008B/2598